IT'S HARDLY WORTH TALKIN' IF YOU'RE GOIN' TO TELL THE TRUTH

IT'S HARDLY WORTH TALKIN' IF YOU'RE GOIN' TO TELL THE TRUTH

TED STONE

Western Producer Prairie Books
Saskatoon, Saskatchewan

Cover illustration and design by Warren Clark/GDL

Second printing 1989

Printed and bound in Canada

The publisher acknowledges the support received for this publication from the Canada Council.

Western Producer Prairie Books is a unique publishing venture located in the middle of western Canada and owned by a group of prairie farmers who are members of Saskatchewan Wheat Pool. From the first book in 1954, a reprint of a serial originally carried in the weekly newspaper *The Western Producer,* to the book before you now, the tradition of providing enjoyable and informative reading for all Canadians is continued.

Canadian Cataloguing in Publication Data

Stone, Ted, 1947–
    It's hardly worth talkin' if you're goin'
to tell the truth

    ISBN 0-88833-188-6

1. Tall tales—Prairie Provinces.   I. Title.

GR113.5.P7S77 1986   398.2′09712   C86-098017-0

Contents

For my parents and my children

Acknowledgments

Until this century, storytelling, the telling of oral tales, has been an integral part of almost every society's culture and history. In recent years, at least in North America, we've tended to ignore that tradition. Radio and television, movies and home video games have all taken over much of the time we've traditionally devoted to conversation and storytelling.

In rural areas, too, old-fashioned storytelling has come on hard times. Electronic entertainment, while more recent in the countryside, has conquered the heartland almost as completely as it has the cities. A remnant of the old tradition, much stronger than can be found in urban areas, hangs on there, but when you talk to rural people today you are more apt to hear about grandfathers or grandmothers who were storytellers than you are to meet contemporary practitioners of the art.

Despite its current difficulties, though, storytelling won't quite die. Storytelling clubs, festivals, and even schools are springing up all over the continent. There's a magic in oral tales that people refuse to give up, that nothing else can duplicate.

I've lived in rural places for most of my life, and for all of that time I've known and listened to storytellers like Sparky Anderson, the man I've portrayed in this book. While much of what Sparky has to say here comes from my own life and imagination, a large percentage of his stories have come from people who have learned of, and shared, my fondness for storytelling.

This book contains tales I've learned not only from members of my family, friends, and neighbors in the town where I live, but also from people who are, or once were, strangers to me. It's these people, who have cared enough about storytelling to contact me by letter or through various readings and radio programs I've done, that I especially thank for the contents of this book.

It's Hardly Worth Talkin'

Yes, sir, I know a little bit about this town all right. I've lived here all my life. Just the other day, in fact, one of the Hawkins boys told me I was the oldest man in Deer River. I told him that I didn't know about that, but if it was true, I sure didn't have any desire to pass the job on to a younger man. Getting old ain't so bad anyway, especially when you stop to consider the alternative.

Oh, I know some of these young kids around here call me "Old Windy" when they think that I ain't listening. I guess they figure I talk too much, and tell too many of them old yarns.

As far as that goes, I guess there were people who thought that even before I got old. Sarah, my wife, used to tell the kids that I had the best memory of anybody she ever knew. She said that I could remember things that never happened. Sarah always laughed when she said that, though, so I know she only pretended that she didn't like for me to be a-telling them tales to the three young ones. When you get right down to it, I think she really liked hearing them stories herself, even if some of 'em were made-up.

I'll tell you something, I learned an important lesson about

1

life when I was just a young boy. I couldn't have been more than about eight or ten years old, but one night at the supper table I told my family a little story. It didn't amount to very much, just some little incident that happened at school that day I thought was worthwhile telling.

It was a good enough little story, but my Grandpa Anderson took me aside after supper and explained something to me that day that he figured every kid ought to learn. I can remember him putting his hand on my shoulder, and saying, "Sparky, do you know, it's hardly worth talkin' if you're goin' to tell the truth."

And I've never forgotten my grandpa's advice. See, he knew that with just a bit of work my little story could have been a lot better. Grandpa used to say that, no matter what you had to do in life, you should do it with all your might, 'cause anything worth doing at all was worth doing right.

"Good enough just isn't good enough," he'd say. And, just like anything else, he figured that if you were going to tell a story you should make the best job of it that you can, even if it means stretching the truth a bit once in awhile.

And I want to tell you, my Grandpa Anderson could tell some whoppers. I was only about twelve years old when he died, but I can still hear him telling them yarns of his about all the things that he used to do when he was young.

He had an unusual accent, Grandpa did. He spoke sort of proper, something like an Englishman.

I can see him just as clear as if it was yesterday. He'd lean back in his rocking chair on the front porch there and say, "Well, now, sir, that reminds me of the time...", and then he'd go into some long, outlandish tale of one kind or another.

He was always fighting about six men at once, and coming out on top. The worst of it was that he expected you to believe what he said, no matter how ridiculous it was. If you didn't, why, he'd get mad as the blazes at you, or at least act like he was.

I remember him telling me once how he used to hunt bear with a baseball bat, and he said that he used to catch wild geese in the fall of the year with nothing but a fishing line and a number six hook. Grandpa said catching geese was easy. He'd just poke a fish-hook through a kernel of field corn and then toss his fish line up onto this ridge out behind his house.

See, Grandpa used to scatter so much corn up on that ridge that it became a regular feeding spot for every goose that came through the area. On mornings when Grandpa wanted to fish for wildfowl, he'd just cast his fish line up towards the center of the ridge and it wouldn't take more than a few minutes before a big old gander would come along and grab that bait slick as you please.

Then it was just a matter of reeling that goose in. "Yes, sir," Grandpa used to say, "I've caught more geese that way than most people will ever see in a lifetime."

Grandpa said that he used to catch the odd duck that way, too, but he'd always throw it back. He said ducks were just too small when you were used to catching geese.

I remember Grandpa told me that one October he caught so many geese one particular morning that he had a whole wagon load of 'em to take to town to sell. He said that to keep 'em from getting away, he tied all of their feet to the cover rope that ran along the sides of the wagon. Grandpa said that when he got about halfway to town, though, this big old gander stood up and started honking and flapping his wings.

Well, that got the whole works of 'em so excited that, before Grandpa could do a thing about it, that wagon load of geese all started squawking and beating the air with their wings. Pretty soon, of course, the wagon lifted right up off the ground and them geese flew away with it. Grandpa said that he was just able to jump clear in time, or else he'd have been taken right along with 'em.

He said that the next spring he kept a-watching, but that wagon never did come back north. He'd always look over at me real serious after he finished telling me that story and say, "No, sir, Sparky, I never laid eyes on that wagon again—and it was a pretty expensive outfit too." He said the horses alone were worth a thousand dollars.

Do you know, years later I heard Dad tell the same story as if it happened to him. Only when Dad got to the part about the geese flying off with the wagon, he claimed that he got his foot caught in the brake while he was unhitching the horses, and the geese took him right up in the sky along with the buck-board.

Dad said that he got back down by releasing one bird at a time so that the wagon gradually got lower and lower in the sky. He said that he figured out how to steer that rig, too. He just had to be careful which side of the wagon he let the geese loose from.

See, if he wanted to go a little to the left, he'd untie one bird from that side. And if he needed to make a sharper turn, he'd release one or two more birds from the same side at the same time. If he wanted to go to the right, he'd do the same thing on the other side. Dad said once he got on to it, he enjoyed himself so much up there that he just flew around the countryside for awhile, before he finally decided to come the rest of the way down.

Then, when he got the wagon down low enough, he was able to jump out. By that time there were only five or six geese left so he was able to pull the wagon down after him, too, even though them geese were still trying to fly away with it. Dad said the closest call on his whole trip was when they were flying over Delta Marsh and hunters started shooting at him.

I liked the alterations Dad made to Grandpa's story all right. But I still always liked Grandpa's version the best; I suppose 'cause I'd heard him tell it first.

That man was sure something else when it came to talking, let me tell you. My granddaughter, who works for the college in Winnipeg, keeps trying to get me to tell some of them old yarns into a tape recorder, but I tell her my Grandpa Anderson was the one who should have done that. I guess I never paid close enough attention because I've forgotten most of them tales he used to tell. He was one of a kind all right, but do you know, it used to be people just told a lot more stories to each other than they do nowadays.

I've lived in this town all my life so I know. My folks bought a little farm on the edge of the sand hills south of town here and they moved up into this country just a few months before I was born. To most people that pretty well makes me a native.

'Course, there's some people that'd say you've got to have

kinfolks born to a place before you can really be part of it. Tom Hannah said that just living in a town wasn't as good as being born in a place where your parents and grandparents were all raised.

Tom said that he had a cat one time that had a litter of kittens in his wife's oven, but being born in there didn't make them kittens homemade bread. To Tom it was the same with people. I don't go with that, though. It doesn't matter where your parents come from. Everybody's got to have a place where they're used to living.

Take Jake Peters, for instance. He was darn near full grown before he came out here after the first World War. He was so poor that he came to town wearing about six pairs of trousers and you could still see his arse, but Deer River got to be his home just as much as anybody else's.

Jake was some relation to old Horseshoe Miller, I think. At least it was Horseshoe who got him to come out here from Manitoba. Jake came here to work in Horseshoe's blacksmith shop, and to play baseball on the Deer River team.

Jake was a great baseball player. He played third base, and he could hit anything anybody could throw. See, baseball used to be pretty important here in Deer River back when I was a young man, and knowing Horseshoe, I expect that's why he wanted to hire Jake to begin with.

After Horseshoe gave up the blacksmithing business, it was Jake who bought him out. That was in the 1920s, just after the government closed Horseshoe's little export store selling whiskey to American bootleggers.

Jake's old blacksmith shop used to be just down on Second Street. Donnie Arnsted owns the building now and he has it fixed up into a little service station and welding shop. It looks pretty good too, a lot neater than when Jake had it. The shed where Horseshoe used to store his whiskey was right across the road, but they tore that down forty years ago—maybe more.

Jake never had anything to do with that whiskey business anyway, unless maybe he helped Horseshoe load some of them American trucks. See, back in Prohibition times, American bootleggers used to come through here in the middle of the night to load up with whiskey and then go back across the line, driving with no lights, watching out for the border patrol.

I don't really know why they bothered being so sneaky about it. There weren't any real roads from here going down into Montana or North Dakota back in them days, so there wasn't that much chance of getting caught. Maybe in some of the bigger places farther west, but not out of Deer River.

For the most part, people didn't even know we were here. They still don't, for that matter. We're kind of in a little backwater here all by ourselves, and it was even more that way back in the days before the government put in paved roads and everybody got automobiles.

Grandpa Anderson

Oh, this was quite a little town back in the old days, I'll tell you. We had a bit of everything around here: cattlemen, farmers, bootleggers. We even had a murderer from Texas stay all night at the hotel once back in the 1800s, and Grandpa used to tell me about Sitting Bull and his men coming through this part of the country after they whipped Custer down in Montana.

Grandpa loved telling stories like that about the early days of the west. In his stories he was always right in the thick of things, and he claimed to have been good friends with lots of famous people, like Sam Steele and Gabriel Dumont.

I guess I was only four or five years old when Grandpa Anderson came to live with us. He'd been all over the world by that time, according to his stories at least. As far as that goes, I believe he really did go to most of them places he talked about. A lot of his tales might have been made up, but he couldn't have told 'em with so much detail unless there was some truth in 'em. And if he did just ten percent of the things he said he did, why, he would have still done more than an average man could do in two lifetimes.

Grandpa wasn't a big man the way Dad was. I guess he'd

have been average height, but he had a willowy kind of build that made him seem small even to a young boy.

He slept in a little lean-to addition built off the back of our kitchen, and I remember how, every morning, he'd draw a pitcher of water from the well and then take it into his room to wash. He'd be up early, but he wouldn't come out until Mom had breakfast on, and by that time his face would be scrubbed red with the cold well-water.

Grandpa was born in Massachusetts, but he ran away from home when he was only about twelve and I can remember him telling me that on the day that he turned sixteen years old, he was working on a freighter, going back and forth across the Atlantic Ocean between New York City and Cape Town, South Africa. The boat was one of the early steam ships, and Grandpa was what they called a fireman. That meant he shoveled coal. Grandpa said that he worked sixteen hour shifts on that boat, just shoveling coal steady, and between shifts he'd only get six hours off to sleep before he had to start a new shift again.

The worst of it, though, was that there was a man with a bullwhip who paced back and forth on this walkway that ran above the boiler room. He'd never say anything to anybody, but if you slowed down your shovelling any, Grandpa said this guy'd whip you 'til you shoveled fast enough to suit him.

Grandpa always said that he'd spent some lonesome birthdays in his lifetime, but there'd never been any as miserable as the one he spent on that boat. He said that he just figured life had to be a lot better than that, and when he got back to New York City he decided to go out West and be a cowboy.

According to Grandpa, at one time or another he'd lived and worked all over the West. He told me once that he'd been on the last cattle drive to leave the Texas panhandle for Kansas City, and he talked a lot about Mexico and California, too.

Most of Grandpa's stories, though, seemed to originate around Calgary or Great Falls, Montana. He said that he worked once for an iron mine near Butte, Montana, hauling ore from the mine to the closest railroad, which was half a day's drive away by team and wagon. He said the land was so hilly, and the load so heavy, they had to use these big long teams of mules to do the pulling, since horses just couldn't stand the weight.

You've seen them commercials for Twenty Mule Team Borax haven't you? Well, them mule teams would be nothing compared to Grandpa's outfits. He said out there at that mine they had the longest mule-trains the world has ever seen.

Why, he claimed that to make just one trip with that ore, he'd have to hitch so many mules to the wagon that it'd take him three hours to buckle all the harness in the morning. He said that there were so many mules in one train that on most of the trail the swing team would end up wading through about six inches of mule manure.

Grandpa said he'd always be real careful checking his animals over in the morning before he left, because he knew they'd be going up and down over these real steep hills all day long. He said the hills were so close together that most of the time he'd still be coming down one of 'em while the lead team would be just going over the crest of the next one. He said that once he got into the hilliest part of the trail, and the lead team had gone over the top of the first rise, why, he wouldn't lay eyes on 'em again until he got to town.

Of course, being a cowboy, Grandpa did a lot of rodeoing, too. At least he did until one time at the Calgary Stampede, when the bronc he was riding on got his foot caught in Grandpa's saddle stirrup. Grandpa said he looked down and saw that horse's foot in the stirrup and said, "By damn, if you're a-getting on, I'm a-getting off." He claimed to have jumped clear of that horse and given up rodeos for life.

Grandpa loved the Rocky Mountains and he claimed to have been a hunting guide out there for awhile. He used to tell all kinds of stories about cougars, and bears, and all sorts of other animals, too. I remember he used to tell about these mountain sheep that they used to have out there that are extinct now. This particular kind of sheep lived in such steep terrain, that over the generations, they evolved legs that were shorter on one side of their body than on the other. Grandpa said these sheep were able to get around on the mountain slopes better than anything except birds and snakes. They'd just keep their short legs on the high side of the hill and walk around and around the mountain as they grazed.

These sheep were kind of a novelty animal, though, and big game hunters from down East started shooting 'em. I guess it didn't take too long after the hunting started before they'd killed off all but two of the poor critters.

The government tried to save that last pair but it turned out that all they had left to work with was a clockwise-grazing ewe and a counterclockwise-grazing ram. The ewe ended up eating her way up the mountain where she starved to death at the top, while the ram ate his way down the mountain and was never seen again.

Before they went their separate ways the animals did breed, though. The rangers had to help 'em along with it, I suppose. It didn't turn out too well anyway. The ewe had a pair of twin lambs the spring before she died, all right, but they turned out to be nothing but trouble. What with having mixed parentage the poor little guys weren't right. One of 'em had two short legs on the front and could only graze going up hill. He finally died at the top of the mountain with his mother. The other one had two short legs on the back and couldn't graze at all. At least that's the way Grandpa said it happened.

Grandpa always claimed to be the best hunter to ever walk the woods, and the best shot too. He used to tell a story about one time when he was hunting moose up in the Waterton Lakes area. This was back before it was a park. He said that on this particular day he came up on the east shore of the lake, and he could see a huge moose with trophy antlers standing on the other side. Grandpa said that it was just standing there wading around in the lake, munching on the water lilies.

Now, Grandpa told me that he had an awful long shot to do it, but he fired and dropped that moose with a clean hit right through the heart—and an old muzzle loader was all the gun that he had to shoot with. Grandpa said that after he shot the animal he headed out for what he knew would be several hours of hiking around the lake before he could get to his moose.

It was a hot day, though, and as he walked, Grandpa got to thinking about how that meat was liable to spoil around the wound before he could get there to dress the animal out. The more he thought about it, the more he figured he should do something, so finally he decided to double back to the spot where he'd shot the moose originally. He loaded up his rifle with powder, and packed it in real good. Then, instead of using a lead bullet, he tapped in several pieces of rock salt, aimed, and shot that moose right in the same spot he'd hit it before.

Of course, the salt cured the meat so there was nothing wrong with it when Grandpa finally got around the lake to clean his moose. "Yes, sir," he'd always say after telling me that story, "I could really do some shooting in them days."

Another tale Grandpa told about hunting with a muzzle loader took place up in northern Saskatchewan way back before the turn of the century. He said that he was out on a hunting trip one time and ran right out of lead shot. He still had a gun full of powder, though. It was about forty below zero outside and he was on his way back to camp when all of a sudden a grizzly bear came charging out of the woods.

Well, Grandpa said it scared him so bad that he broke out in a cold sweat, but the weather was so frigid the sweat froze in little beads right on his forehead. He said that he hardly had time to think, but as fast as he could he scraped them beads of frozen sweat off his forehead, tapped 'em into his gun, and fired. Of course, the explosion melted the ice so it came out of the gun in streams of water.

But the air was so cold that the spraying water immediately froze into little pointed icicles. The icicles pierced the bear's head, and when that happened, the bear's body heat melted the ice again and the bear died of water-on-the-brain.

Grandpa said the bear fell dead right at his feet. He always claimed that was the closest call with a bear he ever had, except for the time down in Montana when a black bear jumped right on him.

He said that when that happened he'd been trailing the bear for several miles, but the animal must have got wind of him, because it doubled back and ambushed him from behind a boulder as he walked past. Grandpa said that the bear jumped right on top of him, but when it opened its mouth to bite him, why,

Grandpa just stuck his hand right down the bear's throat and grabbed him by the tail and turned him inside out.

Another time Grandpa told a story about a bear chasing him through the woods. He'd been out cutting fence rails when a big black bear took after him. Grandpa said he tried to escape across the clearing in the forest where he'd been cutting young aspen trees, but the bear was too fast for him. I guess the only way Grandpa saved himself was to grab one of them fence rails on his way past, swing it into an upright position, and climb to the top of the pole to get out of the bear's reach. Then, Grandpa said, all he had to do was run the bear off by beating the critter with the other end of his pole.

Yes, sir, there wasn't much Grandpa couldn't do. Or at least there wasn't any story he couldn't tell. Grandpa had lots of tales about snakes, especially snow snakes. I don't think there's any snow snakes around anymore, but back in Grandpa's day there were lots of 'em. Snow snakes were only active in the winter, of course, on account of their coloring. See, they were all white on the top and green on the bottom. In the winter they'd be crawling around in the snow everywhere, but they'd hibernate all summer. They'd just lie on their backs out in the grass, and nobody would even notice they were there.

Grandpa also had a lot of stories about hoop snakes. In fact, I think he was the first one to ever tell me anything about 'em. In this one story I remember, he told about how he first came up to this country from the Dakotas in an old Red River Cart. He said one day when he was all alone out in the middle of the prairie he drove over a big badger hole and broke one of the wheel rims on his wagon.

Well, Grandpa said he tried to fix it, but it was broken beyond repair so he got this idea to use a hoop snake to fix the rim. A hoop snake is a snake that will roll itself into a hoop and roll along the countryside like a loose bicycle tire.

Of course, Grandpa's first problem out there on the prairie that day was to catch a hoop snake if he was going to fix that rim. He'd always been a great fisherman, and he never went anywhere without taking his fishing tackle along with him, so Grandpa decided to see if he couldn't catch a hoop snake on a fish line. He was always catching unusual critters with his fishing gear.

Anyway, Grandpa caught a little tree frog to use for bait, and then he cast his line out into the tall grass next to the wagon. Nothing happened there, so after awhile he cast his line out in a different direction. He still didn't get anything, though. Finally, after about twenty minutes of trying, he cast his line into the tall grass over to the opposite side of his wagon and he got a little bite. He said it was just a little nibble, but he cast out that way again and sure enough he brought in a hoop snake.

Unfortunately, it was too small to go around the wheel, so he had to throw it back. As it turned out, he had to catch three more hoop snakes before he finally got one big enough to fit.

You have to handle hoop snakes real careful, on account of 'em being so poisonous. Grandpa did all right, though. A hoop snake is just like a turtle. Once they bite something, they never let go of it until the sun goes down. If you're trying to use 'em for a wheel rim the trick is to get 'em to bite their own tail. Once you do that, why, you're away. They won't let go until dark.

Grandpa got his snake to go into a hoop without too much trouble, and he fitted that hooper over the wagon wheel just as slick as you please, so in no time at all he was off across the prairie again. Grandpa was trying to make it to some little town he knew was nearby while he still had daylight, but just as the sun was beginning to set, that hoop snake let go of his tail, slid off the wheel, and bit the wagon tongue. Then it crawled off through the high grass. Grandpa said that he should have known better than to have put the patched wheel on the front of the wagon like that, but by the time he thought about it, it was already too late.

Of course, without the snake there substituting for a rim, the wheel fell apart right away. Grandpa said it wasn't until he got down to look at the damage, though, that he noticed that the wagon tongue had been bit. He said the wood had already started to swell by the time he noticed it, and when he went to lance it, he couldn't find his hunting knife.

Grandpa was only a little way from town at this point, though, and so he decided to go for help. It was only about a mile, but do you know, before he could get back with the blacksmith, the poor wagon had died. Grandpa always said that he just wished that he'd have cut the tongue off to keep the poison from spreading. He said that if he had done that he might have saved his wagon.

Bert, Woody, and Skinner Fry

I remember one story Grandpa told to me about a woman who drowned herself right here in Deer River. It was up at the horse trough that they used to have on Main Street.

Years ago, see, there used to be an old well with a hand pump up in front of the bank building. It was meant for people to water their horses, but lots of folks who didn't have good wells of their own used to come here to get water for their homes, too.

Oh, I guess that pump was here right into the 1950s. Might have been pretty close to 1960 before they ever got around to taking it out.

The woman who drowned herself came from a family named Hawthorne, who used to live on the edge of town here, out past the railroad tracks, up on land owned by Will Maystead now. It happened when I was just a little kid, so I don't remember it myself. I only remember Grandpa telling me the story about it.

This lady had about twenty kids, and a drunkard husband who was as mean as a mangy dog and not near as good looking. One night after everybody had gone to bed, the poor woman just walked up town here, and laid down in the horse trough and drowned.

I guess the whole family moved away after that, 'cause I don't remember meeting any of 'em. But Grandpa told me all about what happened. He said Skinner Fry found the body.

That Skinner. He might have been a couple of crackers short of a barrel, but you couldn't have found a friendlier person in the world. And he was funny, too, in his own way. I remember him telling me once, how he'd almost killed himself one time when he was out rabbit hunting in his back yard.

See, Skinner had this little twenty gauge shotgun that he couldn't seem to get the hang of, and one day he happened to see a rabbit run under the back porch of his shack. Well, Skinner went to get his shotgun, and then he chased the rabbit back out into the yard. Of course, that rabbit was heading for the fence just as fast as it could run, and Skinner had to shoot in a hurry. He said that he thought he got the bunny in his sights, but when he pulled the trigger, why, he missed the rabbit and hit an old pair of pants that was hanging on his clothesline.

Skinner said that was the closest call he ever had with a gun. He said that pair of pants was shot right full of holes, and by golly, if he'd been a-wearing 'em, he'd have shot himself in the hind-end.

I guess back when he was alive there wasn't a day when Skinner Fry missed being the first one in town to walk down Main Street in the morning. Oh, sometimes a stray dog or cat might have beat him to town I suppose, but most days when he'd come around the corner by the hotel and look down the road towards Woody's barbershop, Skinner'd find himself all alone.

Most of the time he'd just wait in the alcove in front of the hotel for somebody else to come along before he'd go on up to the barbershop. Sometimes it'd be me that'd show up next, but usually it was Wally Conklin.

Wally used to run Bascum's General Store, and as soon as Skinner would see him tapping on the barbershop's front window, why, he'd start out for Woody's, too. By the time Skinner would get to the barbershop, Woody would have made it down from his apartment upstairs and be opening the front door.

Wally'd grunt some kind of greeting at him, and then follow Woody to the back of the shop, tossing a coin or two into the tip dish as he passed it. Skinner'd fall in behind, but Woody never charged him anything.

Woody was no more talkative than Wally first thing in the morning, so Skinner would never say anything either. He'd just stand there waiting for Woody to open his supply cabinet.

Woody would sit in that old captain's chair, fumbling with his keys like he was a banker getting ready to lend money to somebody he wasn't too sure of. He'd lean over slow and put the right key in its hole, breathing heavy the way he always did, on account of all the extra weight he carried.

Only after Woody got the cabinet door open and had fished out that quart jar of Harry Doyle's homemade whiskey—and the three of 'em had drunk a little glass of it—would anybody talk. The whiskey seemed to be the signal for Woody and Wally that the day had started.

Woody'd pour himself a second glass, and some mornings Wally would too, but Skinner'd never ask for more than one. I guess he was afraid Woody might charge him for it.

Sometimes Woody'd get his barbering tools out of the cabinet after he put the whiskey jar back inside, but usually he'd just leave the cabinet door ajar and stay in his chair by the mirror, talking. Once he got started, of course, it was hard to shut Woody up.

Skinner'd sit across from him in one of the chairs that lined the wall. He liked looking at the cartoons at the back of the *Field and Stream* magazines Woody used to leave out for his customers to read.

Wally would never stay long enough to sit down. He'd stand at the window, talking for a little while, and then go down the street to open his own store, Bascum's old general store.

Some mornings there'd be other people who'd come in and join Woody in a drink, too. I used to do that once in a while myself if I got to town before Bert was open in the morning, and so did Jake Peters, and sometimes Tom Hannah too.

I guess that if you get right down to it there was no telling who might show up. I suppose at one time or another almost everybody did. And so far as I know, those morning get-togethers provided the only money Woody's tip-dish ever saw—except maybe for the donations of salesmen passing through town.

Some mornings Woody would get to teasing Wally about being so short, and whenever he did that, Wally would get so mad he'd leave right away. Actually, Wally wasn't all that short, but when Woody found out that he was sensitive about his height, he wouldn't leave him alone. I remember one time when he told everybody that Wally was suing the town for building the sidewalk so close to his arse. Wally got so mad, his face turned red, and I was waiting for the steam to start coming out of his ears. He just huffed off to open his store instead, though.

Another morning I remember, there was about a half a dozen of us there in the barbershop when all at once we noticed Skinner sitting in his chair looking at an old newspaper. I think it was the *Hastings Gazette*.

Now Skinner couldn't even read his own name and he had this newspaper upside down. We were all kind of chuckling about that when Wally said, "Hey, Skinner, is there any interesting news in there?"

Now it happened that this paper had a picture of a brand new automobile on the front page. The new models had just come out for that year.

Well, Skinner shuffled the pages a bit when Wally asked him what was in the news, and then he said, "Naw, there's not too much interesting in here today."

Then Skinner paused, scratching his bald head and looking at the upside down picture of that car. He wrinkled up his forehead so you could see that he was thinking pretty hard about something. Then he said: "They've had a bad car wreck someplace, though."

Most days, by the time Bert Gibbons went walking by the barbershop's front window, Woody's morning tea service would be just about over. Skinner would usually look up when Bert went by and say, "Well, there goes the boss. It must be seven o'clock."

Skinner's comment was just about as dependable as Bert was. Bert ran the local coffee shop in town. His cafe was next to Woody's barbershop, right where the new credit union is now, but Bert and Woody didn't get along.

See, at one time they'd been in business together. In fact, it was Bert who taught Woody how to cut hair in the first place. That was after Woody married Irene. Her sister Louise was Bert's wife so Bert and Woody were brothers-in-law, although you'd never get either of 'em to ever admit to that.

Neither Bert or Woody were from Deer River originally. Bert came here from New Cambridge and Woody grew up on a farm over near Sparta. Bert was the one who started the barbering business. It was right in the building where both of 'em ended up working. When he first started, Bert had a lot of extra room in there, and so after Woody and Irene got married, he rented them the apartment above the shop and taught Woody how to cut hair.

See, Bert was thinking he could make more money if he worked a couple of chairs instead of just one. Woody learned real quick too. In fact, he got to be the better barber of the two.

The partnership didn't work out, though. Deer River just ain't a two chair town. And with all that time waiting for hair to cut, Bert and Woody got to arguing, and the first thing you know they ran a partition through the building and made it into two barber-shops. Bert owned the building so he got the biggest half of it, but Woody got the apartment upstairs 'cause he was already living in it.

To make ends meet, Bert started selling sandwiches, and when that business turned out to be pretty good, he built an addition on the back of his shop and put in a card room. That pretty much left the hair cutting to Woody—although Bert kept his chair right at the end of his lunch counter, and for years afterwards he'd give you a trim whenever you wanted one. Woody turned to selling moonshine to supplement his income. He didn't sell a lot of it really, just enough for a little extra cash. Most of the time he was just a barber.

Skinner Fry, though, that's who I started to tell you about, he used to begin every morning with a shot of Harry Doyle's moonshine at Woody's. It was a social occasion for him, something he could look forward to when he went to bed at night. Skinner just liked to be with people.

Of course, that morning shot of whiskey was tonic to get

Woody and Wally through the day. Either one of 'em would eat a bale of hay if you'd pour a little whiskey on it. Woody used to tell me how he knew that he wasn't an alcoholic because he never took a drink after going to bed at night nor before he opened up his shop in the morning. He thought that was some kind of achievement, but as the years went by, it got so you didn't dare go for a haircut at Woody's if it was much past lunch time.

I remember one summer afternoon when Pete Hawkins came into Bert's after a haircut at Woody's. It was kind of comical listening to him explain to Bert why he hadn't come to him for a clipping in the first place. Pete's hair was in such a mess Bert had to cut most of it off so that it wouldn't look like a buzz saw had got ahold of him.

Skinner Fry did odd jobs around town all his life, at least from the time I can remember anyway. He never had any family, just lived all by himself about a mile out of town. He was a dependable sort, though—just so long as you provided lots of extra instruction, and didn't expect anything done in a big hurry.

He used to work for Bert a lot, washing dishes or anything else Bert would come up with for him to do. Bert told me once that Skinner was a good worker, but he didn't like for him to have coffee breaks 'cause it took so long to retrain him afterwards.

Another time I remember Bert telling about how he tried to send Skinner over to New Cambridge with two big boxes of cheese for an uncle of his named Charley Rice. Bert said he gave Skinner the keys to his truck and was watching him carry the boxes of cheese out the back door when he figured he'd better check and see if Skinner still remembered where he was headed.

Skinner didn't have any trouble remembering that he was on his way to New Cambridge, but when Bert asked him who it was he was going there to see, well, Skinner just got a perplexed look on his face. Bert could tell he was having trouble remembering.

"Now, you just take your time and try to think, Skinner," he said. "Remember, the man you're going to see has the same last name as something they eat in China."

Well, Skinner thought for a minute, and then he said: "Chop Suey?"

The thing about Skinner I've been a-trying to tell you, though, is that in the end he fooled us all. You know, that man did nothing but odd jobs around town here—working for meals at Bert's, or sweeping up sometimes at the auction barn.

The farthest he ever got from home was that time we all went to the baseball tournament up in Moose Jaw, and that didn't cost Skinner anything. Some mornings, Josh Peterson used to give him a nickel to sweep the sidewalk in front of the hardware store, but it seemed like that was about all the cash money Skinner ever saw.

Everybody tried to help him out. He just lived in an old shack built on a road allowance outside of town so he didn't even own his own land, and he was never dressed too well so people used to give Skinner their old clothes when they thought he might be able to use 'em. In the summer people used to bring him vegetables from their gardens, too.

Anyway, Skinner got older and finally died. He was already way up in his eighties, maybe even nineties, by that time, and he was healthy as a fat cow right up to the end.

One morning he just didn't show up at Woody's and when they went to check on him they found him dead in bed. The thing was, though, they found an old nail keg there beside him filled with pocket change—nickels, dimes, quarters, and fifty cent pieces, no pennies. Lots of them coins was as old as Skinner was too. And sewn in his mattress they found another three or four thousand dollars in bills.

All together, Skinner's money totaled more than five thousand dollars, and in them days five thousand dollars was a lot of money. People who used to give Skinner clothes and things to eat didn't have near that much cash and they all wondered how Skinner ever got ahold of so much.

The answer was easy, though. Skinner never spent a nickel that he didn't have to, and in Deer River people saw to it that he didn't have to spend too many nickels.

Coffee
and
Conversation

I guess if there was any one place in Deer River where people told stories more than any other it was up at Bert's. His old cafe was only about fifteen feet wide, but it was thirty-five or forty feet long, so you could jam a lot of folks in there.

Bert had an old oak serving counter that ran most of the length of the restaurant and people liked to sit along there if they could find room. There was about a dozen of those stools with the round seats that spin when you turn on 'em.

I'll tell you though, most mornings you were doing good at Bert's just to find an empty spot to sit down, even at one of the tables he had for the overflow. Why, likely as not there'd even be somebody who didn't need a haircut sitting in the barber chair at the end of the counter.

Bert opened up right at seven every morning and the place would be full before eight—and it'd stay full darn near 'til noon, with maybe just a couple of slow periods. It wouldn't be the same people in there the whole time. As one person would get up to go to work, somebody else would sit down in the empty chair.

Even with all that traffic in there I don't think Bert sold much of anything except coffee in the morning. He wasn't much of a

23

breakfast cook so people just came to sit around and talk before they went off to do their day's business.

'Course, if you wanted something in Bert's besides food, your chances were pretty good for finding it. Nowadays, you'd probably call Bert's place a convenience store, not a cafe. He sold a little of everything in there, from shotgun shells to headache pills.

He sold fishing gear, too, and I always thought it was kind of comical the way Bert kept angleworms in the refrigerator right along side of his sandwiches. And like I said, he'd give you a haircut, too, if you wanted one.

By about nine or nine-thirty every morning, the early coffee drinkers would have pretty well cleared out and Bert would usually have a little bit of free time before people who worked in town would come in for their mid-morning dose of coffee. 'Course, nobody in Deer River had an official coffee break, but you couldn't tell it 'cause around ten o'clock every day Bert's would fill up again. Milt Moyer would lock up the post office for half an hour every morning about that time, so I guess that's what got people into the habit. After the ten o'clock crowd left Bert would get another rest before people started coming in for dinner at noon. Bert always had a special of some sort or another at the noon meal.

In the afternoon Bert did a pretty steady business too. He'd get the coffee break crew between two and three, but there were always other people coming and going too. Lots of days the card room alone was a full-time enterprise. Bert had a half a dozen tables back there, and an old pool table too.

Nobody but the kids paid too much attention to the pool table, but Bert rented decks of cards and cribbage boards for a nickel a match and there always seemed to be a game or two going on. It seemed like about half the time Bert would be in one of the games himself. They played euchre a lot in there too, and sometimes the card games would last right up until Bert closed for the night, even on weekdays.

Conversation was the main form of entertainment at Bert's, though. People would sit in there and swap one tale after another. It was just natural to 'em, part of what conversation was all about. After all we didn't have television or video games for entertainment back then. We had to make our own amusements.

That was the thing about sitting in Bert's every morning. You could always count on hearing an entertaining story. And of course, there was always gossip to catch up with.

See, people told all kinds of stories in there, but they talked mostly about the people who lived right there in town. Some of what you learned even turned out to be true, once in awhile.

Pete Hawkins always used to say that Deer River didn't need any newspaper 'cause a person could find out all there was to learn about our town just sitting having coffee in the morning with Bert. He'd never mention the fact that a lot of what you learned in there was just stories, though.

Old Horace Wagner knew about the stories all right, but he also knew Bert's was the one place in town where he could be sure of finding a good audience, and of course, a good audience was what Horace wanted most. Talk about your storytellers, Horace Wagner was the Member of Parliament in this riding for about thirty years, and you can't survive in that business for that long without being able to tell a tall tale or two once in awhile.

Horace was born and raised on the other side of Austin, but I doubt that he had ever set foot in Deer River before he ran for office. After he was a politician, though, you'd have thought he was an old home boy the way he carried on whenever he came to town. Old Horace wouldn't come here very often, and he'd only stay for a few minutes each time, so he had to make the time he had count. That's why he'd usually arrive in the morning and go straight to Bert's.

I don't know if it's true or not, but they used to say that when Horace would come back from Ottawa, he'd land at the airport up in Hastings wearing a fancy suit. Somebody would be there to pick him up at the airport, and he'd change his clothes in the back seat of the car on his way out to visit all the small towns. I do know he always wore work clothes when he came into Bert's, and he talked just like he was one of the boys.

Everybody liked Horace all right. I guess they figured even if he was a crook he was at least our crook. Besides, he could tell a funny story when he wanted to. That'd make anybody a popular fellow in Bert's.

I remember one time when he told us about the best hunting dog he ever owned. Horace said that dog was such a good tracker, he was able to chase down a coyote after finding the animal's footprint in a concrete section of a five year old sidewalk.

He said that the dog only got confused on that old trail once. See, the dog tracked the coyote through one of Horace's pastures and all of a sudden he stopped right in the middle of the field and started running back and forth like he couldn't get to the other side of something. Horace said that at first he couldn't figure out what the dog was up to. It was obvious that the dog still had the scent, but the poor hound just held his nose in the air, and kept running up and down the field, like he was wanting to climb over something that wasn't there.

About that time, though, Horace figured out what the trouble was. See, there'd been an old rail fence right in that spot that Horace had torn down two years before. He said that he figured the coyote must have ran up and down the fence trying to confuse his trail, and the dog just had to sort out the smells.

Horace said the dog was so smart, though, it only took him a couple of minutes to get everything straight. He said the dog finally worked his way over the fence and caught the coyote before nightfall.

Horace said that dog worked harder hunting than any dog he had ever known. He said that he took the animal rabbit hunting one time up in the Goose Mountains and the dog retrieved five wounded rabbits at the same time. The way it happened was that they were walking along the edge of a little meadow when all of a sudden six rabbits dashed out the end of a hollow log. Horace said the rabbits startled him so bad he let loose with both barrels of his shotgun, right into the middle of 'em.

The dog, of course, instantly gave chase and scooped up a wounded rabbit in its mouth. When Horace called the dog to come out of the high grass, though, it wouldn't come. He said he called and called, but the dog just stood there in the grass wagging its tail and holding the rabbit in its mouth. Horace said the dog had always come when it was called before that, so he figured something must be wrong. He walked out into the meadow and here the dog had four more wounded rabbits, one under each paw.

Horace told another story about this same hound. He said that the dog got turned around on a trail one time and tracked a six year old timber wolf all the way back to its birthplace. Horace said he lost that dog by letting it out for a run one night by itself. I guess the dog treed a bear and then starved to death, waiting for Horace to come along and shoot the critter.

Another time I can remember Horace telling about this hired man that used to work for his dad. I guess this fellow had the biggest appetite of anybody you've ever heard of. He ate so much that one time at harvest Horace's dad got to bragging on how much he could put away, and he ended up betting the threshing boss ten dollars that the man could eat a whole calf.

Well, they got busy and butchered the animal, and then took it to Horace's mother to cook. She figured that if somebody was going to eat a whole calf, she better fix it up as appetizing as possible, so she baked all that meat into pies.

They brought the hired man in and started feeding him those pies all right, but after eating about half of 'em, he started saying he couldn't eat no more.

"What are you talking about?" Horace's dad said. "I've seen you eat more than this lots of times before."

"Well, I know it," the hired man said, "but this time I've got to save room for that calf."

I can remember one time how Horace was telling everybody how when he first started flying he hadn't liked airplanes very much, although he said that he'd finally gotten used to 'em from riding back and forth to Ottawa all of the time. He said that he wasn't scared a bit anymore. In fact, he said that he'd already fallen out of an airplane once, and it didn't even bother him.

Of course, everybody got after Horace then, asking him what he was talking about, falling out of an airplane. "Oh, yeah," says Horace, "I was just lucky that I landed in the sand hills south of town here. See, I came down in that sand, and buried myself so deep in it, that I had to walk three miles for a shovel big enough to dig myself out."

Yes, sir, that Horace told some interesting tales all right, but there's been lots of different kinds of stories told in Deer River over the years, lots of serious ones, and lots of sad ones. The ones

I always liked the best, though, were the ones people told just for fun—like the story Pete used to tell about this wren. He claimed to have watched the bird building a nest in the front pocket of a pair of his bib overalls one afternoon.

The overalls were hanging on the clothes-line and Pete said he just happened to look out the window in time to see a little wren with something in its mouth land on the line and then dart into the pocket. A minute later the bird flew away again. In a couple of more minutes, though, it was back again, carrying a little twig in its beak.

Pete said that he got so interested in watching that wren build her nest that he stopped working and spent the rest of the afternoon watching the bird. Pete said he learned a whole lot about bird life, just sitting and observing.

He claimed that the most amazing part was that whenever the bird would bring back a stick that was too big to go into the overalls' pocket, why, she'd just break it over her knee and take it inside cut in half.

I've listened to Pete tell that story so often that I could say the words along with him as he talked, but the glow never went out of his eyes when he told it. It reminded me of Jake Peters when he used to tell about that hailstone of his. See, we had a bad hail storm here back in the twenties and for years afterward whenever anybody would bring it up Jake would tell 'em about the hailstone that hit his shop.

He was just like Pete was with his story about the wren. He'd get this gleam in his eye every time he told it. And he told it every chance he could get, too. Jake claimed the hailstones from that storm were so big and hard that one of 'em went right through the roof of his shop.

Jake said that it didn't stop there either. He said that hailstone kept going right through the upstairs floor and it still fell in the shop below with enough force to put a dent in his anvil when it hit it.

I've heard old Jake tell that story a hundred times if I've heard him tell it once. People in Bert's would always laugh when they heard it, though. That's all that mattered to Jake.

Jake Peters
and the
Johnson Brothers

Yes, sir, it used to be that if you wanted to hear a story in this town all you had to do was stop into Bert's for awhile. I guess practical jokes were the other main form of entertainment there. People were always willing to go a fair distance out of their way to play some kind of a foolishness on each other, like that time when Tom Hannah piled horse turds in front of Josh Peterson's hardware store.

See, Josh was a pretty fastidious fellow. People always said he should have been a banker. He used to wear a white shirt and neck-tie every day of the week, and every morning he'd sweep the dirt from the sidewalk and street directly in front of his store.

His hardware shop was across the street from Bert's, so peo-ple had been a-watching Josh sweep dirt for years before Tom got the idea one afternoon of dumping a gunnysack of horse drop-pings in front of the store.

I don't know what made him think of it, but most everybody in the cafe could see the humor in his little scheme. Tom went on home and loaded a bag of manure from old Dobbin into the back of his truck, then he came back to Bert's and played euchre

29

until after it got dark, and Josh had gone home for the night.

Harvey Arnsted helped do it. They dumped the whole sack load as close to Josh's door as they could get it, and still make it seem like a horse left it there.

The next morning there was standing room only at Bert's, and Woody's barbershop was full, too. Josh cleaned up the mess when he saw it, though, and never did come in for coffee that day.

The following morning, though, it was all people could do to keep from laughing when he came into Bert's, and started complaining about Morley Parker driving his horses in town. "This is the twentieth century," Josh said. "They shouldn't allow that kind of stuff no more."

After that Tom would leave a sack of road apples in front of the hardware store whenever he took the notion, and Josh cleaned 'em up for two years before Skinner Fry told him the truth one time by mistake. People figured Josh might actually shoot old Tom, but instead Josh bought a truck load of stall cleanings from Oscar Hoppingarner, and took 'em out and dumped 'em right in Tom's front yard.

That should have been the end of it, but Tom Hannah—being his usual self—just let that manure pile sit there on his lawn. When Josh saw how his pile didn't seem to bother old Tom, he got twice as mad as before. He fumed to himself for a few days and then went out and got another truck load, and dumped it right on Tom's front steps.

That spurred old Hannah to action. He cleaned up both piles. Later he told everybody that he didn't really mind a manure pile on his front steps since he always used the back door anyway. Tom said that he was just afraid that if he didn't clean it up right away, Josh would dump another load in his living room.

Yes sir, people used to pull some ornery jokes on one another. Do you know, though, I think one of the meanest tricks anybody ever pulled backfired on 'em.

It was when Jake Peters got the Johnson brothers with that story of his about government money in black spruce seed cones. See, Ab Johnson and his brother Simon were always pulling pranks on somebody or other, and one time they did kind of a bad one on Jake.

They had an old 1936 Ford pickup truck and neither of its windows would roll down. To make matters worse, the driver's side door didn't open from the inside, so when Ab drove it to town he had to climb across the seat and get out the passenger side.

Anyway, one day the handle on the passenger door broke off, too, and Ab and Simon got this idea of locking Jake inside the truck. See, with the passenger door handle broke off, there was no way to get out of the pickup if you shut yourself inside.

Ab and Simon drove all the way to town with the doors open, parked the truck in front of Jake's shop, closed the doors like there was nothing wrong, and then went in and asked Jake to weld a new handle on the passenger side. Jake said that he would do the job just as soon as he got time, and Ab and Simon said they'd come back and pick up the truck later in the day.

All they did, of course, was go down the street to Bascum's store and watch out the window until they saw Jake come out to drive their truck into his shop. As soon as they saw him close the door they started laughing and telling everybody in the store what had happened. Everybody watched Jake drive the truck into his shop, and then stood there for awhile, speculating about what they'd do if something similar happened to them.

After Ab and Simon figured Jake had been in there long enough to suit 'em, they walked down to his shop to get him out. By the time they got there, though, Jake was just climbing through one of the truck's door windows.

He'd used his pocket knife for a screwdriver to take the door panel off and then he just pulled the window glass down from the bottom. Ab and Simon made a big show about being sorry. They said they just figured Jake had known about the driver's door not being able to open.

Jake took the whole thing real well, not knowing he was the butt of a joke. He told Ab and Simon not to worry about it, that he was used to climbing out pickup truck windows.

Then he welded a new door handle on the passenger side, and after that, since he already had the panel off, he fixed the window and door handle on the driver's side to boot. He didn't even charge 'em for that either. It wasn't until after the Johnsons had left that somebody came in and told Jake that he'd been had.

Jake laughed at himself, and never did say another word to Ab or Simon about it. A few weeks later, though, Jake was sitting in Bert's when Simon came in.

The two of 'em talked about the weather and what not for awhile, and then all at once Jake says, "Well, Simon, I guess you and Ab will have pretty well cleaned up the seed cones on that spruce ridge of yours by this time."

Now of course, Simon didn't know what Jake was talking about. And when Jake told him the government was paying twenty-five dollars a bushel for black spruce seed cones he just about fell off his chair.

"Oh, yeah," said Jake. "They're buying 'em to start some kind of reforestation project, but you've only got a week before the pick-up date comes for this area. They'll only take 'em next Friday morning at ten o'clock up at the Pool elevator in New Cambridge."

Well, I wasn't there at the time, but Jake told me Simon left Bert's without even drinking his coffee. See, the Johnsons owned about a quarter section of black spruce trees and the seed cones were thick that year. At twenty-five dollars a bushel they were set to make what for them days would be a pretty good sized piece of money.

Ab and Simon worked that whole week bagging spruce seeds even though they had lots of other work they should have been doing. They spent so much time working in the woods they never saw anybody else, so nobody ever told 'em that Jake had fed 'em a story.

Jake never thought they'd go as far as they did without finding out the truth, so he was pretty surprised the next Friday morning when Ab and Simon drove up to his shop with a three ton truck full of black spruce cones. They'd come to ask him where it was they were supposed to sell 'em.

Well, at that point Jake figured they'd kill him if they found out the truth, so he acted real sorry and told Ab that he'd made a mistake about the black spruce cones. He said that the government had all the black spruce they needed and only wanted northern pine cones for the time being. Ab and Simon were pretty disappointed about their lost fortune, but they drove away without nailing Jake's hide to the outhouse door. Jake told me the whole story afterwards.

The funny thing about that tale, though, is that the very next year the government did start buying black spruce seed. Ab and Simon still had their cones, too. They'd kept 'em in an old granary over the winter and when the Department of Natural Resources started advertising for 'em in the spring, they sold the whole works for good money.

I was in Bert's the day Simon came in to thank Jake for telling him about it in the first place. Jake just smiled and never did let on about the way it really happened.

The First Liar
Never
Has a Chance

That Jake, he was something else, I'll tell you. I just wish some of these young kids who call me Old Windy could have heard him tell some of his stories.

Somedays, sitting in Bert's or over at the old hotel, he'd get going like he was never going to stop. I especially remember them crazy yarns he used to tell about the weather that they had back when he was a kid growing up in Manitoba.

Why, I remember him telling one time about a storm back there that left so much snow on the ground that the landmarks for miles around were buried. He said that you could walk along the river valley and all you'd see would be the tops of the trees sticking up above the snow.

Jake said that he lived up on a high spruce ridge, but that winter the snow was so deep that when he'd leave the yard he could drive the team out onto the prairie just as if it were on the level. He said that the snow was so deep that year that he had to keep a path to the chimney shoveled so the smoke could get out.

One day he went to town for supplies, and while he was in the store a chinook blew in, and all that snow started to melt.

Jake said that he came out just in time to save his horses. See, he had 'em tied to what he thought was a hitching post, but it turned out to be a telegraph pole and his team almost got hanged when the snow melted down closer to ground level.

Jake said that as soon as he saw how fast the drifts were melting away he figured that he had better head for home as quick as he could. His family's farm was east of town and for awhile he drove along, keeping just ahead of that warm air coming in from the west.

Little by little, though, the weather began to catch up with him. Jake said that as soon as he began to feel the sunshine on the back of his neck, he knew that he was in trouble.

Pretty soon he saw that the snow under the sleigh was melting. Jake had four horses in his team, and he said that he tried to make 'em go faster but the front pair had to buck about three feet of snow all the way.

It wasn't long, though, before the second pair was running in the mud, and I guess the sleigh itself rode across bare ground most of the way home. And it threw up so much dust the dog running behind suffocated before he got halfway there.

Now I'll tell you the truth. I've seen lots of snowstorms, and even a few chinooks in my day, but I never seen any like Jake's. And cold weather: why, to hear Jake tell it, nobody had cold weather like they did back where he came from.

He said that most winters it'd get so cold that it would freeze the nuts off a bridge. And one year Jake said that it was so cold that two or three times over the winter he saw magpies towing ravens, trying to get 'em to start.

Jake told me once that sometimes during the worst of the cold spells they'd have to use kerosene in the car radiators instead of antifreeze. Even then the cars wouldn't go unless you put parkas on the hood ornaments first.

Jake used to say that it got so cold back in Manitoba that two or three times every winter, the smoke in the wood stove would freeze and plug up the chimney. He said one time it got so cold that a tub of hot bath water froze solid right next to the kitchen stove, even though there was an oak fire burning with both dampers wide open. Jake said it happened so fast he only had time to get halfway out of the bathtub before the water froze. He claimed it took him two days of sitting by the furnace before all the ice melted off his foot.

Another time Jake told me about a winter so cold the thermometer froze up and busted. He said that he went out to call the cows back to the barn, but even though he called and called, they wouldn't come home. See, I guess his words were a-freezing just as fast as they came out of his mouth and them cows never heard him. Jake said it was so cold that winter, those words never thawed until spring, and then they all melted on the same day and he had cows coming to his yard from all the neighbors' farms too.

He said that kind of thing wasn't really all that unusual. In fact, he said that lots of times when he was a kid him and his brother would lie in bed talking, and late at night, after the fire had died down, it'd get so cold in the house that their words would start to freeze.

He said that whenever that would happen, he and his brother would try to talk for a while before they'd just give it up and go to sleep. But then the next morning when they'd build a fire in the living room stove, all them words from the night before would thaw out at once. Jake said that it'd get so noisy in the house that everybody would have to go outside to get away from it.

Another year it got so cold out there that Jake said that the air froze. He said that if you went outside then you had to use an icepick to breathe.

Jake said that as cold as it got that winter, though, the lakes still weren't safe enough to skate on. He said that the ice worms were so thick that year, that you couldn't find a place big enough for a hockey game where they hadn't weakened the ice with all the holes they'd ate.

Winters used to come on in a hurry back then too. Jake told me about one year when they set a record for autumn turning cold the fastest. He said that when he went to bed in the evening the weather had been so hot the cows had been giving pasteurized milk, but when he woke up in the morning there was snow on the ground and all of the stock tanks were frozen solid. He said that the last splash of water coming off the pump had frozen right in the air so that when it hit the ground it killed a mouse who'd just come along there for a drink.

And the lakes. Jake said they'd frozen over so fast during the night the ducks and geese hadn't had a chance to fly south first. They were frozen tight in the spots where they'd been swimming the day before.

He said that on one of the lakes there had been a big brown trout that had just jumped after a dragonfly when the cold snap came. Jake said the frigid weather came so fast it caught that fish in mid-jump. Of course, when the trout came back down on the lake, the water had already frozen and the fish landed on the ice. Everything turned out all right, though.

See, the fish hit his head on the ice when it landed and got a big gash just above its eye. And all the blood from the cut melted a hole in the ice for the trout to swim back into the lake. Jake said the next morning he could see the marks on the ice where it had happened.

I remember Jake telling another story about cold weather. This happened on a night when he'd come home late from a dance. According to Jake, when he pulled into his yard his pickup truck stopped with a jolt just as if he'd hit a concrete wall. He said that he started the truck up again, but the vehicle wouldn't move anywhere, forward or backward. Everytime he'd try it the engine would kill.

Jake said that he had to think about it for awhile before he realized what had happened. He had a parka on the hood ornament okay, and there was lots of kerosene in the radiator, so he couldn't see why the darn truck wouldn't go no matter how cold the temperature was.

But I guess what happened was that when he turned into his driveway, his headlights had shone up against the side of the house and they had frozen solid right there. The truck couldn't move. Jake told me that he had to get the crosscut saw and saw the light beams in half before he could get the pickup truck the rest of the way into the driveway.

No, sir, they just don't have weather like that anymore, let me tell you, but do you know, the funny thing about Jake telling all them cold stories was that he really couldn't stand cold weather at all. He hated it. 'Course, he'd never admit to that. But he never spent any more time than he had to in winter weather, either. His shop was only about a block from Bert's, but in the winter he used to drive his truck over there whenever he wanted to get a cup of coffee.

When it came to talking, though, Jake just had to outdo everybody else. "The first liar never has a chance," he'd say after you'd tell him a story, and then he'd tell you one just a little bit bigger. He had a name for them tales of his. I think he called 'em "plausible impossibilities."

Like that time when I was bragging about my garden doing so well. I told Jake my sweet corn was ten feet tall. I told him my garden was on the west side of the house and the corn was so tall, the sun went down every night two hours earlier than usual. I said it was so big I had to cut the stalks down with a crosscut saw.

"Oh, that's nothing," Jake said. "My corn has grown as high as the roof of my two storey house."

I didn't like getting beat in a story, so I said, "Come on there Jake, how're you going to harvest a crop like that?"

Jake just looked at me and said, "Why, from the upstairs window, of course."

Jake had me again, but I kept trying, though. I told him the ears on my sweet corn were so big, six of 'em filled a gunny-sack. Jake just smiled and said none of his corn cobs would fit in a gunnysack, even after they'd been shelled. "I was out picking corn borers off the stalks the other day, though," he said, "and I was able to get one of them into a bushel basket."

By this time, I'd already given up, but Jake went on to tell me about his zucchini squash crop. He said it was the only thing in the garden that hadn't turned out too well. "The zucchini were big enough all right," he said. "But the darn vines grew so fast that they wore holes in the squash, dragging 'em across the garden."

Another time I had this made-up story about a sow I owned that didn't have any back legs. I told Jake that I'd fixed her up with a little cart made out of a plank and an old set of roller skate wheels. I told him that I'd strapped the cart under the hog's rear end to help her get around. I claimed that after she farrowed, this sow had fourteen little pigs all with her with their own little carts.

Jake just grinned when I told him that story and started telling a tale of his own about a pet hog he'd had once. It was an orphan pig who'd been raised by the family dog. Jake said that it turned out to be such a good rabbit hunter, that they'd have probably kept it if they'd been able to break it from its habit of chasing cars.

After that Jake came right back with a yarn about a cat that he used to own that had lost a hind leg in an accident with a mowing machine. Jake said that he fixed that animal up with a nice wooden leg to take the place of the real one.

"And do you know, Sparky," he said, "that cat turned out to be a better hunter than she'd ever been. After I fixed her up she'd sneak up on the mice just like before, but then she'd whack 'em over the head with her wooden leg."

I remember once when Pete Hawkins was telling a real whopper that ended with him climbing up a tall tree and driving a spike into the moon. Jake told Pete that he believed that story because he'd seen the nail up there. "In fact," he said, "it was me that clumb up there and clenched it."

Another time we were all standing around in Jake's blacksmith shop, telling hunting stories that kept getting bigger and bigger. I remember Pete telling how he'd gone out to this real mountainous region hunting bighorn sheep one time and he claimed that the land was so steep out there, that when they'd get up in the morning they'd have to squint up the chimney to see if there was any sheep around.

Anyway, we got to talking about duck hunting and Jake comes out and says that one time he killed 99 mallards with one shot. Everybody groaned with that one, and I said, "Come on, Jake, why don't you just say that you shot an even hundred?"

Well, Jake just looked at me like I'd hurt his feelings. "Why, Sparky," he said, "do you think I'd lie for the sake of one extra bird?"

Moose Meat
and
Smoked Oysters

Now I know darn well Jake had planned to suck somebody into helping him with that little gag of his about the ducks right from the start. But I don't know yet how he got me to do it. It reminds me of a story he told to a bunch of us boys one day when we were all standing around his blacksmith shop passing time.

It was about a moose hunt that he went on back before he came out here. He said that his family back home in Manitoba was real poor, and when he was growing up they had to look after everything pretty careful, since they couldn't afford to be spending money at the store all the time.

Jake said that they were always able to eat all right, though, since wild game was usually real plentiful back where he came from. He said that sometimes they'd go hunting and scare up so many rabbits at one time that the critters would run over each other trying to get away.

Jake said that a couple of times he's seen rabbits running in circles so thick that about half of the bunnies would be a-crashing head-on into each other. Jake said that you'd just have to stand there watching 'em for a while, and then all you'd have to do for a rabbit dinner would be to go pick 'em up where they'd fallen after they'd knocked themselves out.

Jake said that one time back in Manitoba he chased a squirrel into a hole in a big oak, and when he got to looking at that tree, why, he could see it moving. There was a crack in the bark along one side of the tree, and Jake said that he just sat there watching that crack open and close. He said it was down-right eerie, just watching it.

And he couldn't seem to figure out what was going on so he went and got an axe to cut down the tree. And do you know, that oak turned out to be hollow, and it was packed so full of animals that the crack in the bark had been opening as the animals inhaled, and closing as they exhaled. Jake said he was able to capture enough meat from that one tree to last until Christmas.

Late in the winter when it'd come time to go out and get some more game, Jake said he and his brothers used to take turns going hunting with the family's only gun, an old Winchester shotgun with an octagonal barrel made in the 1800s. He said that to save money, nobody was allowed to leave the house with any more than two shells, a slug for big game and lead shot for birds or rabbits.

He and his brother had a deal worked out in case they shot something too big to carry out of the woods alone. See, if either one of 'em killed something that was too big to carry home, they'd shoot the shotgun shell to signal for help.

Jake said that one real cold winter day it came to be his turn to go for meat. It was about forty-five below zero with a bit of a wind coming out of the north, but he took the shotgun, and his two shells, and went outside anyway. He said that he put them shells in one of his mittens.

Jake went a little way and saw some rabbit tracks, but he figured a rabbit was just too small. He said he figured that he should get more meat than a rabbit.

He went a little way farther and saw a deer track. He was going to follow the deer's trail, but then he remembered that his brother had shot a deer the last time he'd gone for meat, and Jake just figured he could get something a little bigger than his brother could get. He went along a little farther, and he found an elk track, so he decided to follow that trail.

After he had followed the elk's path for a mile or two, though, he came to a spot where a moose had crossed over the same trail. Jake figured the moose track was fresher, and he also figured a moose was bound to be a lot bigger than an elk, so he decided to switch trails. By this time he was getting a long way from home, and it was getting kind of late in the afternoon.

Jake said that he followed that moose trail for about an hour before he caught up to the moose. By this time, it was almost dark, but Jake said he could see the moose real good through some poplar trees on a little ridge.

He said that he was just about as close as he figured he could get, so he decided to shoot. He pulled off the mitten where he had put his two shotgun shells, but it was so cold his fingers were a little clumsy and he dropped both of 'em into the snow.

Well, Jake found the slug all right, but he couldn't find the other shell. The snow was too deep. And it was getting darker all the time so he took his one bullet and shot the moose.

According to Jake, it was an excellent shot, and the moose dropped in his tracks. Then Jake had a problem, though. He didn't have that second shell to signal for help, and of course, there was no use even attempting to carry that moose home by himself.

Jake said that he went over and cleaned the moose right away, though, and then he skinned it out. Afterwards he built a big fire and cooked up a little piece of that moose meat for supper. Since it was already dark it was too late to go home, so after his supper Jake just sat around the fire trying to keep warm.

He said that it was so cold that night that every time he cut wind his farts would freeze. He said the darn things kept him awake, because whenever he'd start to fall asleep, one of them frozen devils would drift over the campfire and explode. He said a couple of 'em sounded like a cannon going off, and one time one of 'em caught fire.

Then Jake said he got the idea that he should use the moose hide for a sleeping bag. It had pretty well dried off there in front of the fire by that time, so Jake climbed inside and went to sleep.

He said that it was warm and cozy in there, too, and he got a pretty good night's rest.

The next morning when Jake woke up, though, the fire had died down, and that moose hide had frozen shut tighter than a locked coffin. Jake said that it was as stiff as a board and it had him pinned inside so close that he couldn't even roll over. He said even his feet were clamped together in that hide, and they were cold from losing so much circulation.

Jake said that at first he thought he would be all right if he could just get his big hunting knife out of his belt. But he was having trouble getting his hands free.

He said he was squirming around in there, trying to reach his belt buckle, when all at once he happened to look through the slit in the hide covering his face, and there by the fire, where he'd left it the night before, he could see his hunting knife.

Well, now everybody in the blacksmith shop was quiet when Jake said that. Then Skinner Fry, who was standing there with his mouth open, said, "My goodness, Jake, what did you do?"

Jake kind of grinned and said, "Why, there was nothing I could do, Skinner, except freeze to death."

Well, everybody laughed at that, of course, but when they stopped, Jake said, "No, Skinner, I'll tell you what really happened that day."

See, I guess the thing was, lying there in that moose hide like that, Jake just figured he was going to freeze to death for sure. He said that he just knew that he was going to die, and when he accepted that, well, his whole life flashed before him in his mind.

When he remembered the previous fall's federal election, though, he got to thinking about the candidate he'd voted for. And Jake said that when that happened, he just felt so small that he was able to climb right out the hole in the hide where he'd shot that moose.

Yes, sir, that old Jake was something else. Another thing I remember him doing is sitting in the beer parlor and banging his empty glass on the table whenever he needed another drink. It'd make Mabel Fisher madder than a wet hen at fly time whenever she was the one waiting on tables. I guess that's why Jake did it. He'd never say a word, just sit there, and bang his glass up and down, until she brought him another beer.

She'd always yell at him to take off his hat indoors too, but Jake wouldn't pay any attention to her then either. He had this old tan hunting cap that I'll bet he wore every day for thirty years. I don't think he ever took it off. He didn't like exposing his bald head. Somebody was likely to tease him about it, I guess.

You know, one time I was in the hotel when Jake came in with a little tin of smoked oysters. I don't know where he got 'em from, but when Walter Maxwell came in a little while later, Jake right away said to him that he'd bet him a beer that he couldn't eat one of them oysters and keep it down.

Well Walter, of course, said just as fast that he could eat anything and keep it down. Jake just grinned then, and fed him an oyster. Walter didn't have any trouble at all swallowing it. He got a big smile on his face afterward and says, "Okay, Jake, buy me a beer."

Jake kind of got a surprised look on his face and says, "Well, I'll be darned, Walter. Do you know you're the fourth guy I've given that oyster to since I've been in here, but you're the only one of the bunch that's been able to keep it down."

Now I'll tell you what. Everybody in the place laughed until we cried. Everybody except Walter that is. He never did figure out if it was true or not.

The
Arctic Cafe

Yes, sir, we sure used to have some good times in that hotel, I'll tell you. It reminds me of the time they took Woody Blackburn up to Hastings to get his gall bladder operated on.

Poor old Woody. They said that when he came to after the surgery he was still a little foggy. He squinted his eyes, and grabbed one of the nurses by the arm like he was trying to get his balance. Then he looked up at her with a confused expression on his face and says: "Am I in the beer parlor in Deer River or the one over at New Cambridge?"

'Course, Woody would have been talking about the old hotel, the one that sits empty uptown here, not the new one they've got down on the highway now. Do you know, to my mind that new hotel is nowhere near as nice as the old one. It's all right, but it's just not the same. Why, I can remember when they built the old one, back about 1920, maybe a little before.

Horseshoe Miller and Jim Lee were the ones who put it up. They built the whole thing from rock they had hauled in here from somewhere down around Medicine Lake, Montana. Of course, the railroads were doing good then. We had three grain elevators operating here in Deer River at that time.

47

They're all gone now, óf course. Our old branch line is one of the ones that got abandoned here a few years back. It's too bad, but I suppose it'll work out all right in the end. See, I've got this theory about everything. I think the whole world runs in cycles. Take right now, for instance. We've got all the buffalo we need and the darn railroads are going extinct.

The old Arctic Cafe down by the train station is still running strong, though. Do you know, I guess I ought to tell you a little something about that restaurant. Everybody calls it the Arctic Cafe now, but I'm one of the few people still around who can tell you how that place got its name.

Two sisters named Alice Barkman and Rhonda Fairweather started a restaurant there way back in the 1920s. Alice's husband, Bob, used to run the livestock auction before he sold it to Charlie Conners. Everybody called old Bob "Growlie," and except for when he was auctioneering he was the quietest man I've ever known. Whenever he talked he spoke so softly that you had to just about stop what you were doing to listen to him.

Alice was just the opposite, though. She talked loud, and almost constantly. She was a good storyteller, too. She was a big woman, not tall, but heavyset, and her eyes just shined when she was a-telling something that she thought was funny.

I remember one year when the grasshoppers were about as bad as I've ever seen 'em. I was talking to Alice, complaining about the hoppers and she said, "I know they're bad, Sparky. I had to put wheel chains on the car to drive through 'em coming to town this morning, and I still got stuck twice. I had to dig myself out with the snow shovel both times."

She said the hoppers were so thick out at her place that they'd already eaten almost everything in the garden, including the rhubarb. She smiled when she told me that one, though, and then added, " 'Course, they came to the back door for sugar before they ate the sourest parts."

Another time—this was years later—Alice was telling me about seeing a moose up in the park. "I'm telling you, Sparky," she said, "that moose was the biggest one I've ever seen. It was so big it had to get right down on its knees to look in the car window."

Oh, but listen to me talk here. I was trying to tell you about the Arctic Cafe. When Alice and Rhonda first opened it they called their place the "A & R Restaurant" after the initials of their first names. The building had been a lawyer's office before they made it into a restaurant. As a matter of fact, it was the only lawyer's office this town ever had. The fellow who ran it, though, moved to Calgary back about the same time Alice and Rhonda were wanting to go into the restaurant business, and since it was right across the street from the stockyards, they figured they could do all right there on auction days.

The first thing Alice and Rhonda did after they bought the place was tack up a big sign over the front door. It had the letters "A" and "R" printed real big while each of the letters in "Restaurant" got smaller and smaller the closer they were to the edge of the sign.

At first the "A & R" was only open on days when there was an auction sale, but as time went on, they started staying open other days too. Business just seemed to get better and better for 'em.

After a few years, though, Rhonda and her husband moved up to Hastings. I think her husband was born and raised up there if I remember correctly. Anyway, after Rhonda left, Alice stayed on running the "A & R" by herself—and since she didn't have help anymore she climbed up and painted an "X" over the "R" on the sign. Everybody laughed about that and started calling the place the "A Restaurant"—at least for a time they did.

As it turned out, though, Rhonda must have been the cook because the food was never as good after she moved away. I remember Pete Hawkins telling me once how, after Alice had taken over the restaurant, he'd brought a few of them "A Restaurant" biscuits out to his pasture pond and fed 'em to his ducks. Pete said the poor birds ate the biscuits all right, but afterwards the whole flock sank and he never saw 'em again.

Alice was pretty hard on her own cooking too. She'd laugh and make jokes about it just like everybody else. I remember one time when she told me that old Growlie had gone and used some of her biscuits for the floor of his barn. I guess he ran out of bricks when he was putting in the aisle way, and so he used a half dozen biscuits from the restaurant to finish the job.

Alice said she could have told him it was a mistake. She said the problem was the biscuits turned out to be a lot harder than the clay bricks, so when the floor started to wear, it left the cooked biscuits a fraction of an inch higher than the rest of the walkway. Alice said it would have been all right if Growlie had just put them biscuits in a corner somewhere, but because they were right in the doorway he kept tripping over 'em whenever he went into the barn.

I guess I don't need to tell you that with cooking like that, it didn't take long for business to go downhill after Alice became the chef. Before long, the "A Restaurant" went back to only being open on auction days. It was about then that some people started saying that the "A" on the sign stood for Arctic since likely as not the food would be cold when you got it.

By the time Alice finally sold the place to Charley and Mary Connors, almost everybody called it "The Arctic Cafe." Charley and Mary didn't care. The restaurant was only a handy sideline to their auction business anyway. Since then I guess that auction, and the restaurant with it, has been sold a half a dozen times, but people haven't ever called the cafe anything but "The Arctic."

A Bull
in the
Hay Loft

That reminds me of another story about cooking I always liked. Pete Hawkins told it to me once. He said that just after he and Mary first got married she cooked a pot roast one night, and before she put it in the roasting pan, she cut off the south end of it. Pete said he watched her do it, and then asked her why. Well, Mary didn't exactly know why, but she said that that was the way her mother always did it.

Now, being so particular about things, the next time Pete saw his mother-in-law, he asked her why she always cut the end off a roast. Well, she didn't know why, either. She said it was just 'cause her own mother always did it that way.

Now that really got Pete to thinking. The grandmother was still alive then so he went to see her. And what do you think? She said the reason that she always cut the end off her roasts was because her roasting pan was so small that she could never get a whole one into it.

Now can you imagine that? It went through three generations just by force of habit.

That's the way it is with a lot of things I guess. Why, I remember one time old Cal Murphey and Clayton Powell got in a big argument. 'Course, that was nothing new. They were always doing that. Clayton and Cal lived right across the street from each other here in town, and Clayton was always big in the Conservative party. Cal was a long-time Liberal, so if they didn't have anything else to fight over, they'd get into it over politics.

They used to sit on their front steps and holler back and forth at each other something fierce. You could hear 'em two blocks away when they'd get going at each other. Everybody used to laugh about it, but they wouldn't stop.

One day I remember Cal was trying to get Clayton to explain to him just what it was that made him want to be a Conservative. Every reason Clayton would come up with, Cal would shoot down. Finally, Clayton just got tired of the whole thing and said, "Now, listen here, Cal, my father was a Conservative, and my grandfather was a Conservative, and so far as I know, even my great-grandfather was a Conservative, so I sure enough ain't going to be anything else."

Well, when Cal heard that he went into a rage. "Why, that's the dumbest thing I've ever heard of," he yelled. "Can't you think for yourself? Why, did you ever wonder what would have happened if your father and grandfather and great-grandfather had all been horse thieves? What would you have been then?"

Clayton thought about it for a minute, and then he said, "Well, Cal, I reckon then I might have been a Liberal."

Yes, sir, Clayton got Cal that morning. But do you know, I know darn well that Cal got his politics from his folks too. I knew his family real well. They were Liberals just like Cal.

No matter what he might say to Clayton, Cal was just like most all of us. We're a lot more of what we are 'cause of our raising than anything we learn on our own. My old Grandpa Anderson always used to say that a colt never lands too far from the horse trough and I reckon that's the truth.

That's probably one of the reasons I came to tell so many tall stories, what with my granddad blazing a trail for me the way he did.

After Grandpa Anderson came to live with us, he used to sit out on the front porch in the evening and talk away to whomever he could get to listen. He used to tell a lot of stories about the old days of the west, but my favorite ones were the tall tales and outright lies he used to tell just as if they were God's truth.

He'd sit there in the rocking chair and just talk on for hours at a time. Every once in a while, he'd look over at me right in the middle of some story and say, "Oh, I'd never lie to you, Sparky." Then he'd go on with his tale.

I remember him telling one time about being the marshall down in this little town in Montana when a bull broke out of its pen at the railroad corrals. Grandpa said that it just happened that he was across the road from the train station at the time, and he saw the whole thing.

The bull took off running right down the main street of the town, and Grandpa took off after him just as fast as he could go. Grandpa claimed to have been an extremely fast runner back in them days. Sometimes he'd even say that he had been on the Olympic team.

Anyway, that day the bull got out, Grandpa said he chased after it so fast that before the bull got to the school yard, he had caught it from behind by its tail. He said that he dug his feet into the ground and jerked that bull to such a sudden stop, it split the poor animal's hide right through the center of its forehead.

Another time Grandpa said that he was out at this big ranch in Alberta looking to buy some cattle when one of the bulls started to chase him. He said the animal gave him a good run around the barnyard a couple of times and then started chasing him around a haystack over by the corral. Grandpa said that he ran around that haystack about three times with that bull right behind him.

The fourth time around, though, Grandpa got just a step or two ahead of the bull and jumped on the top of the stack. The bull thought Grandpa was still in the race, though, and just kept running faster and faster, trying to catch up with him. Grandpa said that bull was running around that haystack so fast that, if he'd have looked up, he'd have seen himself running away. He said the bull was running so fast that at one point he blew a meadow muffin right in his own face.

Do you know, that tale reminds me of a story about a bull that's true. It happened while we were still at the farm south of town here. Dad had this old bull that got too ornery to keep so he decided to ship it. We called the animal Old Dan and he developed such a cussedness that it got so we were scared to go out to the pasture field at night to get the cows.

When we went to take Old Dan to town, though, I guess the ornery devil must have known what we were planning for him, because he wouldn't get into the wagon. We didn't have a ramp back then and we spent that whole morning trying to get the animal loaded. We'd walk him onto this little grassed-over manure pile and then try to lead him up into the wagon box from there.

We just couldn't seem to make it work, though. We'd loaded lots of other animals that way, but not Old Dan. We tried everything from tricking him with grain to trying to push him in from behind, but he was just too stubborn for us. Finally, Dad got this idea to use the rope from the barn's hay sling to lift that bull up off the ground just enough to encourage him into the wagon.

Well, I didn't have any better ideas, so we moved the wagon over by the front door of the barn, and then walked Old Dan over under the hay sling. We didn't use the sling itself, just the ropes. We tied 'em around the bull's middle, being just as gentle as we could since we didn't want to get him any more excited than he already was. Then we went and got this quiet old chore team we had, and hitched 'em to the doubletree to do the work of lifting that bull.

Now, at this point everything seemed to be going so well I began to think we was doing the right thing. That bull was standing there as quiet as can be with the ropes tied around his belly, and I couldn't see why the plan wouldn't work.

When Dad told the team to gid-up, though, the ropes tightened around Old Dan and he let out a bawl like nobody who ain't never heard a sick bull low would believe. It scared the old chore team so bad they took off at a dead gallop.

'Course, that shot Old Dan to the top of the barn where the sling mechanism tripped. And that sent him sailing into the loft just as slick as if he'd been a load of hay. It was so darn comical to see it that both Dad and I sat right down and laughed 'til tears ran down our faces.

When we finished laughing, though, we figured we really

had a problem. We couldn't even get that bull to go in the wagon and now we could hear him stomping around up in the hay mow. Neither one of us had any idea how we were going to get him down.

I thought we might be able to use the reverse of the method we got him up there with, but Dad didn't want any part of that. He said he'd butcher him first and take him down in pieces.

As it turned out, though, we didn't have any more aggravation with that bull at all. We went up there and he didn't seem to be hurt a bit.

Dad put a halter on him and led him around just like a pup. Seemed like Old Dan didn't want any more trouble. To tell you the truth it seemed like he wanted to stay as close to us as he could so nothing more would happen to him.

Now, this was a big old barn we had, with a half floor between the mow and the ground level that we used to keep filled with straw. I cut the hole bigger at the ladder well and Dad piled straw into the corner just as high as it would go. Then he walked Old Dan out of the mow onto this straw pile with no trouble at all.

Once we got him that far I got the wagon and loaded it onto the hay rack that I'd backed up next to the half floor. It made for a little drop, but Dad led the bull off the edge of that floor onto the wagon where we tied him tight enough to make sure he didn't get any ideas about going somewhere else.

After we backed the wagon off the hay rack I told Dad that it appeared Old Dan had turned over a new leaf and we ought to just keep him, but Dad said no. He claimed that any bull you have to get down out of a hay loft just couldn't be trusted.

Turkey Pies
and
Prairie Skies

It wasn't too long after we got rid of that bull that I met Sarah. I used to play baseball back then, and Deer River had a great team that year, better than any team we've had since, that's for sure.

See, we'd beat just about everybody there was to beat from around home here so we arranged to go up to a fair in Moose Jaw to play in a big tournament there. I guess before we left we figured that there was nobody that could beat us.

Just about the whole town went along to see us play, even Skinner Fry. The Community Club had organized a couple of cake raffles and a box social to raise money for the team's entry fee, and Skinner had won a free train ticket up to Moose Jaw with us.

We left on the last day of August in 1923. Back then if you wanted to go to Moose Jaw you had to take the morning train to Hastings and then wait two hours for the Border Express to come back through on its way north. We'd no more than left home, though, when our train hit a bull standing on the railroad tracks west of town. I think the animal belonged to Tom Hannah, although he never showed up to claim the body. It didn't hurt anything, except the bull, of course, but the train stopped so quick that suitcases and lunch boxes flew all over the car. It was kind of funny. Everybody started getting off the train to see what had happened, and I went over to see how Skinner was doing.

Now Skinner must have been up pretty close to fifty years old by that time, but he'd never been on a train before in his life so I thought he might be a bit scared after what happened. I didn't have to worry, though, 'cause Skinner wasn't bothered a bit. In fact, until I came and told him there'd been an accident, he hadn't even known we'd been in one. He said that he just figured trains always stopped that way.

Our train got going again pretty quick after that so we still made it over to Hastings in plenty of time to catch the train north to Moose Jaw. And we ended up doing pretty good in that ball tournament, too.

In fact, I'd bet ten dollars against an empty chop sack that we'd have won the blamed thing if Whirly Johnson hadn't got in an all-night card party downtown the night before our last ball game. We'd made it as far as the semifinals after the second day, but the following morning Whirly never got back to the hotel until after breakfast. I guess the night life was too much for him 'cause he looked a little ragged out there on the mound that afternoon.

See, up until then Whirly had been able to give us a pretty good advantage over any team we'd come up against. Horseshoe Miller was the one who'd found Whirly in the first place. He'd met up with him someplace down in Montana, and got him to come up here and play on the Deer River team for a season.

At one time Whirly had been a professional ball player. He'd played for Philadelphia or Baltimore or some team back in the east. Of course, he was a bit past his prime by the time he came to Deer River. He was fat, and he only had one eye, but Whirly was still the best baseball pitcher I've ever seen. He had a fork ball that was just about impossible to hit, and a fast ball that most people couldn't even see.

The real advantage he had over the batters, though, was a psychological one. It's kind of scary, standing in a batter's box, watching a one-eyed pitcher who could throw as hard as Whirly, getting ready to heave a baseball at you.

Whirly wore a patch over his dead eye, and the way he'd squint at a batter with his good eye was enough to make a person think about taking up another sport. The thing about Whirly, though, was that the vision in his good eye wasn't all that hot either. I was Deer River's catcher and whenever a new batter would come to the plate I'd yell out to Whirly and tell him whether the new guy was a left-handed hitter or a right-handed hitter.

Whirly had good enough vision to know which one it was anyway, but letting on like he didn't would really shake up a man stepping onto the batter's box. Along with an occasional wild pitch, it was usually all it took for a hitter to start thinking more about staying out of the way of the baseball than hitting it.

You've got to give old Whirly credit, though. He almost won that last game for us, even after being out all night like that. It was kind of funny. In the sixth inning when he got into trouble, I went out to the mound and told him to bear down.

And he did. Two of the next three pitches he threw hit the umpire. They were just a little high, but they came in so fast I couldn't hang onto them. After the second one hit him, the umpire was so mad he told me to either catch the ball or trade positions with somebody who could.

I didn't miss anymore, though. The batter hit the next pitch over the fence in centerfield. That was the end of it for Whirly. We lost the game by a couple of runs, but the team that beat us went on to win the championship.

Do you know, though, fate's just like my Grandpa Anderson always said. You never can tell when you're going to get a double yolker. As it turned out, it was a lucky thing for me we lost that tournament. Since we didn't have any more baseball games to play, we got to see the rest of the fair. We looked at all the livestock exhibits, went to a couple of good places to eat, and took in the midway.

I even entered a liar's contest they had going there. This was strictly an amateur bout, though. Politicians, preachers, and other professionals weren't allowed to compete. I still didn't win any prizes, though. Morley Parker won 'em all. He told the judges

some big long tale about going mushroom hunting, and finding
so many toadstools that he didn't know how to get 'em home
with him on his horse. After trying several different ways of load-
ing 'em, he said that he finally just took off his pants, tied the
bottom of each leg closed with his boot strings, and filled up both
pantlegs with mushrooms. Then he snugged up his belt, threw
his britches up on his horse like they were saddle bags, and
headed for home. Morley claimed it was the biggest feed of
mushrooms that he ever ate.

Yes, sir, that Morley was quite a storyteller. I can remember
him telling about one day when he worked in the fields so long
that he was too tired to climb back up into the hay wagon to go
home.

"Do you know, though, Sparky," he said, "I'm so strong I just
grabbed the seat of my pants and threw myself into that wagon
with no trouble at all."

Another time, when Morley was trying to get me to go rabbit hunting with him, he claimed that the bunnies were so easy
to hunt out at his place that half the time they'd chase the dogs.
"And when you cook 'em," Morley said, "why, they'll roll over
and baste themselves."

Anyway, after the liar's contest was finished, Morley and I
went back to the grandstand to watch the last ball game, the one
for the championship. While we were there I got to talking to
a bunch of other ball players whose teams hadn't made it to the
finals either.

This one fellow mentioned that he had a sister who was moving to Austin to teach school later that month. After the game
he took me to meet her. And of course, this sister turned out to
be Sarah. She was at the fair, too, and I was the first person she'd
met who could tell her anything at all about the town where she
was going to live. And of course, I had lots of stories to tell her
about that part of the country.

As the years went by, in fact, I had to remind Sarah once in
a while just how much she liked my tales back when we first
met. I talked on and on that day, and she sat there listening to
me with her mouth open. When I got home I worried for a time
that it wasn't my stories that amazed her so much as the amount

of talking I did, but I made a point of going up to Austin to see her anyway, and the next summer we got married back in Saskatoon, where Sarah grew up. Lots of her relatives still live up there.

Sarah and I bought the old Bowerman place right after our wedding, and we moved out there in about the middle of September. It was tough going the first few years. We didn't have anything to live in but that old log house the Bowermans had homesteaded in way back in the 1800s.

When we moved in, I told Sarah we'd build a new place in a couple of years, but do you know, all three of our kids were born and going to school before we ever got enough money for another one. Even then it wasn't new. It was an old house from here in town, but it was in pretty good shape. We moved it out to the farm with horses. That would have been about 1934 or 1935.

Of course, coming from Saskatoon, Sarah had never lived on a farm before. She didn't have a clue about livestock, that's for sure. She'd never even owned a dog or a cat before she moved out here, but it didn't take her long to get into the swing of things.

My dad gave us twenty-five bred ewes for a wedding present, and my older brother Steve brought us two gilts the day we moved to the farm. Along with a few chickens and a milch cow I bought at the sale yard here in town, that's all the livestock we had to start farming.

Sarah was a little afraid of the animals at first, even the chickens, but she had a way with them right from the beginning. By the next spring when the ewes began to lamb, she was already in charge. And if Sarah couldn't save a lamb it couldn't be saved.

Every spring, for as long as we were at the farm, she kept a box behind the wood stove in the kitchen for weak or orphan lambs. If they were born in the cold and had taken a chill, Sarah would just bring 'em in and stick 'em in the oven until they thawed out. If they were really cold she'd throw 'em in the hot water basin.

We would eventually get most of those lambs back with a mother, either its own or one we could fool into adopting it, but there would always be a few we'd end up having to bottle-feed. After they were strong enough to go outside, it used to tickle me to see 'em following Sarah around. She couldn't even go to the outhouse without a troop of lambs behind her. One year, there were about ten of 'em and they'd follow her everywhere she went.

Sarah had a special knack with animals right from the start, especially at birthing time. It's a lucky thing, too, because I had to be away from home a lot there in the beginning. I'd worked for Harv Conklin up at the feed store for four and a half years before Sarah and I got married, and since it was a pretty good job, I stayed on working for him for another two and a half years after we moved to the farm, just long enough to get some of the bills paid.

One time, just three or four months after Roy was born, we had a prairie fire come through while I was away. As it turned out, the fire didn't hit our place, but it came close. When I got home it was blowing across the spruce bluff west of the house and it looked like it was coming right for us. Sarah had lowered Roy, asleep in his baby basket, into a dry well we had behind the barn, and she was plowing a fire guard around the yard. About that time the wind shifted and the fire moved south of us, but it still made me feel bad about working in town, no matter how good a job it was.

Before I started working at the feed store I had worked for a guy named Harley McBride who had a farm a couple of miles east of Dad's. I worked for old Harley for three years starting when I was only about fourteen years old. And let me tell you, you earned your money working for that man. Now I never minded putting in a good day's work. That didn't bother me. I could take as much hard work as anybody. What used to burn my tail, though, was having to go back and work at night.

I'm not talking about working nights when there was something important to get done. I was always glad enough to go back to work after supper during seeding or at harvest time, or maybe even to finish getting the hay in before a rain or something. But Harley would get us out there working in the middle of the night for anything that crossed his mind.

I worked year round at the McBrides, but Harley used to get Pinky Arnsted to come and work for him during the summers, too. Pinky was a year younger than me and we shared a bed in the McBrides' attic. It was always hot as the blazes up there in the summer time, and cold in the winter. There weren't any windows either, no light at all except for this old coal oil lantern that we took up the ladder with us at bedtime.

I liked working with Pinky, but at the McBrides there was absolutely no place we could go to get away unless we went to bed right after supper. We just about had to do that, too, 'cause if we waited around for old Harley to finish his dessert, why, likely as not he'd rope us into going back to work again before bedtime.

I can see him sitting there at the supper table yet. He had a big pot belly all swelled up like a bloated cow, and after about three helpings of dessert he'd always lean back in his chair and look across the table at us.

"Well, boys," he'd say. "We did a good day's work today. What do you say we go outside and sit on the back porch awhile before bed?"

Harley always wanted to sit on the back porch, 'cause Mrs. McBride didn't allow whiskey or chewing tobacco in the house. Before he came in the door, Harley always made sure he took his tobacco out of his mouth and laid it on the porch railing where he could get at it when he came outside again. He kept his whiskey under a loose board in one of the steps. I always liked sitting on the McBrides' back porch in the evening. I would have liked it, anyway, if I hadn't had to look out for Old Harley making us go back to work again as soon as he took the notion.

The weather would usually be cool just after dark like that, and sometimes we'd hear a whippoorwill call, or an owl. We'd look out past the shadow of their old barn and see the sky and stars behind it. It was a real comfortable place to sit. It would have been, anyway, if we hadn't had to worry about Harley sending us back to work.

Old Harley would get his chew off the porch railing and then reach under the step, get his bottle, and take a big drink of whiskey. Then he'd let Pinky and me have a drink, too, like he considered us his equals, even if we were just young kids working for him. Sometimes we'd just sit there for awhile and then go inside to bed, but when the conditions were right, Harley would get philosophical about how pretty the moon and stars were, and how clear the night was. Whenever we'd hear that, Pinky and I would get this sinking feeling in our stomachs.

"Yes, sir," the old man would say looking up at the sky. "It's so bright and clear tonight I bet we could pick a few more stones in that back field of mine."

The next thing you'd know Pinky and I would be out there in the dark, toting rocks over forty acres of summerfallow. Picking rocks at night was something Harley seemed especially fond of doing. Some nights we'd go out when there wasn't but about half a moon shining down on us and we could barely see where we were walking.

I'll tell you what, though, that crazy Pinky fixed it so we didn't have to pick rocks one night. It was after a day when we'd been a-cleaning one of Harley's stonier fields. I knew there was going to be a full moon that night, and since there was still a half a dozen wagon loads of rocks left on the ground when we quit to go for supper, I figured, sure as water runs downhill, Harley would have us back there in the field carrying stones after dark.

On the way back to the house, though, Pinky said to me that he'd bet his day off against mine that we wouldn't be back picking stones again that night. It seemed like a good bet to me, so I took him up on it.

We went on in and did the chores then, but when I saw Pinky lagging behind on the way to the house for supper, I figured he had something up his sleeve, so I slowed down a bit to see what it was he was going to do.

Now Mrs. McBride kept turkeys and they used to roost on the corral fence by the barn door. When Pinky came out of the barn he never lost a step, but he reached down and scooped up a turkey pile from under this old tom just as easy as if he'd been fielding a ground ball in the outfield. When he got to the porch, he dropped that little pastry right in front of Harley's chewing tobacco.

That night after supper, right on schedule, Harley leaned back in his chair, patted his belly, and suggested we go sit on the back steps. Well, neither Pinky nor I needed any coaxing this time. We followed Harley out, and then sat there waiting for him to reach for his chew.

Usually, reaching for that tobacco was the first thing Harley'd do after he'd sit down on the steps, but for some reason on this particular night he grabbed the bottle first. He took a long drink out of it, and then handed it to Pinky.

"Yes sir," Harley said. "It sure is a pretty night." Pinky tipped the bottle up and then handed it to me.

I started to take my drink, but then I saw Harley reach for his tobacco.

It was just about then I got to feeling sorry for what was going to happen. Harley started to say the light was bright enough we could probably see to load another wagon full of rocks, but he only got about half the sentence out of his mouth when he stopped dead.

It must have taken five or ten seconds from when Harley first realized something was wrong to when the full force of the taste in his mouth reached his brain, 'cause I took my drink of whiskey and had time to hand the bottle back to Pinky before he spit that turkey pie at the stars. Harley jumped up, cussing and spitting, and running at a full gallop towards the pump and some fresh water.

'Course, me and Pinky pretended like we didn't know what was wrong. Harley was so upset, neither of us would've felt like laughing even if we'd have dared to. He was spitting and hollering, and then hollering and spitting, just as fast as he could make his tongue work.

By the time Harley finally figured out that he'd eaten turkey droppings, Pinky and I had both gone to bed, kidding each other about not having to pick any more of them rocks. The next morning, though, Harley got us up an hour early, so we got us a chance to go at them stones after all.

Them McBrides, they were quite a pair, I'll tell you. They fought all the time. If one of 'em said one thing, why, the other one would say just the opposite. It's sure no wonder they never had any kids of their own, I'll tell you that.

I can remember one time when the old fools fought for two days over whether they should hang a strip of flypaper ribbon over the kitchen table or from the beam by the back door. After the second day the house was so full of flies, Pinky hung ribbon in both places, and nobody ever said any more about it. I was sure glad to get a job in town and get out of there.

After working for Harley McBride, having a job in town with Harv Conklin was like being on vacation. The pay couldn't match what you can get today, of course, but at the time it seemed like a fortune to me. I guess I might have made thirty-five dollars a month, which was at least twenty-five dollars a month more than I made working for Harley. I saved enough out of that pay, so that by the time Sarah and I got married, I was able to make a pretty good down payment on our farm.

Do you know, I've thought about it a lot and I think working like we did is a good thing for a family. We didn't work all the time, but when we did, Sarah and I never had to worry about where the kids were—because they were usually home working with us. When I think back to those times now I remember us all together, working in the fields, doing the chores, just sitting around the kitchen table shelling beans.

All three of the kids ended up making a good life for themselves, too, and I think the experience they had working on the farm had a lot to do with their success. None of them stayed on the farm, but I think the farm has stayed with them all of their life.

I always figured that Steve and Majorie would leave home and work at something besides farming, but Roy, our oldest, went to agriculture college down at Guelph and I used to think he'd eventually come back to the farm. He didn't, though. He stayed down east working as a livestock buyer for Canada Packers in Toronto. Steve, my other son, became an aircraft engineer and moved to Montreal, and my daughter, Majorie, went to Winnipeg to teach school.

I've got a whole parcel of grandkids now, and two great-grandchildren. I don't see any of 'em very much since they all live in the east, except for Heather, Majorie's daughter, who lives in Winnipeg. She comes out to see me more than any of the other kids do, and sometimes we still go out to visit the old farm. The house is empty now, of course, but I like to stand on the old front porch and look down the hill, out across the prairie. I think it's one of the best views anywhere.

A Blue Jay
and Two Crows

Oh, I'll tell you we used to have quite a time of it, farming in this country. We always used to call it "next year country." For that matter, I guess they still do.

But I'll tell you what, in my lifetime farming has changed almost completely, a lot more than I could have ever imagined anyway. I grew up working with horses, but today, why, there are farmers who can't tell traces from hames.

In some ways it's better now, but not in all ways. At one time there was somebody living on almost every quarter section around Deer River, but today I don't suppose there's one quarter section in six with a family living on it. I don't think that speaks too well for modern agriculture. If these experts know so much, why can't they keep more people on the farm?

Everybody's moving away to the cities, except me, of course. My granddaughter Heather, the one in Manitoba, keeps trying to get me to move to Winnipeg, but I tell her no. When it comes to cities I kind of agree with my old Grandpa Anderson. He said cities were for people who didn't know any better. He said city people get everything backwards. They like to eat outside and go to the bathroom in the house. And in the winter time, why,

more often than not, you'll find that their noses are running, and
their feet are smelling.

Of course, I wouldn't mind seeing my granddaughter more
often than I do. She works at the university up there in Winnipeg.
She's a doctor of agriculture.

Now isn't that something? I'll bet that you didn't even know
they had such a thing as a doctor of agriculture, now did you?
I'd heard of all kinds of doctors myself, but I never knew about
that one. I guess, though, that if there's anything that needs a
doctor these days it's agriculture. There used to be a saying, "get
big or get out." I don't hear that so much anymore, but it sure
seems like there's been a mess of people who've got out—and
a lot of 'em got pretty big before they left, too.

'Course, I never got too big myself, and I didn't get out either,
least ways not until I retired. I just changed my ways of doing
business a little as I went along, that's all. I'd always had a good
eye for livestock. I seemed to have a talent for seeing when there
was a possibility for profit in 'em, so I just started depending on
that skill more for my living than I maybe would have done
otherwise.

That doesn't mean I haven't had my share of troubles with
animals. I've made some good trades in my life, but I've made
some awful mistakes, too. Take that load of sheep I bought up
at the Langley sale that time. I sure wish somebody else would
have got that bunch. There were two rams in that lot, but neither
one of 'em was any good. They fought steady from first light in
the morning until dark every day. I finally just opened the gate
and let 'em go at it. And do you know what? They butted each
other down the road for better than thirty miles. I had to go get
'em clear up the other side of New Cambridge, and they were
still fighting.

I finally sold the meanest one to Tom Hannah, but both of
'em ran off right after that. Two or three people here in town
claimed to have seen them rams fighting up in the Goose Mountains, but Tom and I never found either one of 'em.

The ewes in that bunch from Langley didn't turn out much
better either. They had fine long wool on 'em when I bought 'em,
but the first night they were home we had a big rain storm. It

rained for three days and three nights after that, too, and it just soaked them sheep right through. On the fourth day, the sun came out all right, but it dried that wool so fast it shrunk up to where there wasn't enough of it left to make it worth sending for the shearers.

It reminds me of a story Pete Hawkins used to tell about his sheep. He said that one year somebody told him that ewes needed to be given iron pills to help 'em make it through the winter. Pete said that he figured it was worth a try, so he got some iron tablets from the vet and fed 'em to his sheep. He said he figured if one pill was good, two pills would be even better, so he doubled the dosage. The next spring at shearing time, though, Pete realized his mistake. Every one of the fleeces from those sheep turned out to be steel wool.

Yes, sir, I guess Pete was even worse off with his steel sheep than I was with that bunch I bought up at Langley. I don't feel too bad about them sheep anyway, 'cause I know there have been other times when my livestock buying has turned out a lot better.

In fact, my son Roy—the one who got to be a buyer for Canada Packers out in Toronto—he said he learned more about animals from me than he ever did at that agricultural college up in Guelph. And he said he learned more about buying and selling, going to livestock sales with me right here in Deer River, than he ever did in thirty-five years of buying for Canada Packers. Maybe I never got rich, but I always got by pretty good. And I never had to pay much income tax either so there's some advantages to my kind of farming.

Now Pete Hawkins was an example of somebody who just couldn't adjust to the times. He was a darn good farmer, but there never was a man as particular about the way he did things, or as stubborn. I'll tell you the kind of farmer Pete was. I remember one time after the war I'd figured out how to make a little money shipping low-weight steers to auction up in Hastings. I told Pete about my little scheme and offered him a chance to get in on the deal with me, but he didn't want any part of it. He said he was in business to sell choice steers, and he wasn't going to sell any other kind.

Pete had a mixed farm—like almost everybody else did back

then—but he was proudest of his dairy cattle. His cows were the best producers around, too, and his milk always had the lowest bacteria count. Eventually, of course, the government made it so you had to have milking machines and bulk tanks to sell class A product. Pete only milked about a dozen cows so buying expensive equipment wouldn't have been worth it for his little operation. It was the same with me. I stopped milking cows altogether about that time, but Pete started selling to a creamery over in New Cambridge. Then he bought more pigs and fed 'em his skim.

Of course, there wasn't as much money in cream as there was in selling whole milk. I can remember going to see Pete one afternoon about this time. I knew things weren't going the best for him, and when I got there I asked him if his luck had been improving any.

Pete grinned and said no. It seems that on top of everything else, he'd been having trouble with hawks getting his chickens. I guess a big red-tail had been flying off with one chicken every morning for a week. Pete didn't have too many chickens to start with so I knew he couldn't afford that kind of loss. I asked him what he planned to do about it.

"It's too late now," he said. "This morning I tied 'em all to a piece of nylon string to keep the hawk from flying off with any more, but when he came along, he got the end of the string and took the whole works of 'em."

Things didn't get any better after that for Pete either. When the creamery in New Cambridge closed, he started trucking his milk all the way to a dairy up in Hastings that made it into ice cream. He only did that for a few months, though, before they remodeled that plant. Then they wouldn't take milk in cans there any longer either.

After that Pete sold his cows, except for the one he milked for the house, and he started growing a bit more grain to make up for what he lost in milk. That didn't work out too well for him either. See, Pete's farm was south of town, out towards the sand hills. Most of his land was as good as anything you could find anywhere, but a couple of his fields weren't meant for anything but pasture. The soil just wasn't good enough.

Pete tried cropping some of the more marginal land for a couple of years, but it wasn't worth it. That end of his farm was just too sandy and Pete never believed in using chemical fertilizers.

I remember seeing Pete one day after he came in from threshing. He'd been out in one of his new grain fields, and he just looked at me and shook his head in disgust. He said he'd never seen such a sparse crop. I guess he'd spent half the morning going up and down that field, and after awhile he started wondering why the combine wasn't filling up. Finally, he said he got down and looked in the hopper, and here was a blue jay and two crows eating the wheat just as fast as it came in.

Pete wouldn't change, though. He kept that farm of his like a park, but he always had his own ways of doing things. He mostly liked the old kind of farming the best. The trouble is his kids all went off and got fancy jobs in other places so he finally sold out and retired.

It reminds me of old Harv Miller. Harv had the worst luck of any farmer I ever knew. It seemed like the poor devil never sold anything when the prices weren't rock bottom. Of course, if he was buying something, though, prices would likely be up. And if there was a hail storm anywhere in the area, you could bet it would hit Harv's crop first. It seems like he just didn't have any luck at all.

I remember this one year when we had rain all through August so there was hardly anybody who could get their crop off. Then September came and the weather just got worse. There was even a snow storm at the end of the month. This was back in the early sixties when a lot of people were getting out of farming anyway, and the poor harvest just made things look worse.

I saw Harv up at the auction barn this one day with his boy, Jim. The snow was still on the ground and I knew Harv must have been feeling pretty low about it. The year before he got only a bit of crop 'cause of a drought in the middle of the season and a hail storm at the end of it. And the year before that he'd lost his barn and a lot of livestock in a fire.

I walked over to where the two of 'em were standing and asked Harv how he liked the weather.

"Do you know, Sparky," he said, "farming just ain't the way

it used to be. I'm beginning to think it's impossible for an honest man to make a living at it anymore."

Once he got started talking Harv just couldn't seem to stop. He went on and on about what a tough way to make a living farming was. He said it was the worst job there ever was. Finally he says, "Do you know, Sparky, sometimes I'd just like to give it all up and move to town." Then he shook his head and looked at his son. "I can't, though," he said. "I got to hang on to the place in case Jim here wants to go into farming someday."

It reminds me of the story of the farmer who took a day off one time so he could just sit on his front porch swing and rest for awhile. He was tired of all the work he had to do. While he was there a car came along the road coughing and sputtering and it finally died right there in front of the house.

The driver of the car got out and lifted up the hood and fooled with the engine. After a little bit, though, he came over to the farmer and asked him if he had a screwdriver that he'd sell him so he could fix his car. The man said he'd give him a dollar for one.

Well, the farmer had a screwdriver all right so he sold it, and the stranger went back to his car, fixed it, and drove off. As soon as he was out of sight, though, the farmer went to town and bought two dozen more screwdrivers, at a price of two dollars apiece. At the check-out counter the store clerk asked him what he was going to do with so many screwdrivers, and when the farmer told him he was going to go into business selling them for a dollar each, the clerk laughed right out loud. "Don't you know you can't make any money selling screwdrivers at that price?" he said.

"Oh, I suppose it won't be the greatest business in the world," the farmer told him. "But I figure the work's a lot easier, and the money's a lot better, than farming."

As for me, I farmed a full section of land, but just like Pete, there was no one to take it on after I got too old. That young Maystead boy—Charlie Maystead's oldest son Tom—bought our place four years ago, to add to the land he already owned. He's doing all right out there I guess, although it's a different farm than when we had it. Tom's got a new house up on the highway so nobody lives in our old place anymore, and as for the farming, it's just straight grain out there now.

'Course, I always put in some grain myself when Sarah and I had the place, but most of what I grew I just fed to our animals. I'd sell a little wheat every year, but that was all. My real living came from the animals I raised and the horses I traded—and buying and selling cattle and hogs, of course. I always made out all right with hogs.

It's one thing to know how to buy livestock, but selling right is just as important. I was always traveling around talking to people. I enjoyed doing it, but it also gave me a chance to find out what folks were interested in buying.

That's what I always tried to tell Sarah. I wasn't wasting that time I spent visiting everybody. See, when I bought an animal, most of the time I'd know ahead of time where I was going to sell it. That was just part of my business.

It seemed like I was always on the lookout for something for somebody. Why, I'd go to livestock auctions sometimes three or four times a week, and during the summer I'd go to farm auctions too. You've got to know what you're doing at an auction sale, I'll tell you. You've got to have an eye for animals—and auctioneers too.

It's not that I ever knew an auctioneer to come right out and cheat somebody, unless, of course, it was absolutely handy to do it. It's just that at an auction sale you've got to live by your wits, be on your toes. It's definitely buyer beware territory, I'll tell you that. And that's fair enough, too. After all, you've got to remember that it's an auctioneer's job to get you to buy, and a good one will do it. That's what he's there for.

Old Charlie Conners was as good as anybody I ever knew at getting you to part with a dollar. He ran the sale at the livestock barn here in Deer River for years. I remember one time when Oscar Hoppingarner brought this old swaybacked horse into the sale, and Charlie bragged it up so much that when the bidding ended, Oscar wouldn't sell the animal.

It made Charlie madder than all get out. "What's wrong with you anyway, Oscar?" he yelled. "I know for a fact that the bid is higher than what you gave for that horse."

"That might be true," old man Hoppingarner said, "but after what you said about him, I think I'd be a fool to let him go so cheap."

Another time Tom Hannah brought in a cow that used to kick to beat hell. Everybody knew about it so Charlie couldn't really ignore the problem. It was a good enough cow, but I never did see an animal that liked to kick people so much. Tom said that cow would wait for two or three weeks without kicking once, just so you'd let down your guard, and she could get a good shot at you. He said that if she'd have had claws she'd have scratched like a tiger, and if she'd have had the right kind of teeth she'd have bit like a crocodile too.

Two or three people around here had owned her before Tom and she was the same with them, too. When she came into the auction ring that day, Charlie just sat there behind his little window for awhile and watched that cow run in circles. Finally he anounced to everybody that she was a good cow, but she was a kicker.

Well, everybody knew that already, but Charlie made it out like he was wanting to make sure he wasn't misrepresenting the animal any. He said that he didn't want anybody bidding on her unless they could handle cows.

Well, saying that just about assured him of at least a couple of bidders. Charlie had made it a matter of pride, and three or four fellows started bidding right away just so everybody would know that they could take care of livestock.

Finally it got down to just Walter Maxwell and Harry Arnsted doing the bidding, and it looked like Walter was going to let Harry have it, which was surprising since Walter didn't like for anybody to get the edge on him when it came to big talk. The price was already high enough for her to have been a decent cow, though, so maybe that's what was scaring Walter off.

Anyway, that's when Charlie stopped the auction for a minute and said to Walter that he had Harry's bid, and he thought that Walter ought to let the cow go. "She'll take somebody that knows what they're doing to manage this one," Charlie said.

Well, that was just as much as telling Walter that he didn't know how to handle cows. It didn't take but about two seconds for him to come in with another bid and the whole thing went a couple of more rounds before Harry gave it up and let Walter have that old milker.

Now I didn't want any part of the bidding on that animal. Charlie wasn't selling a cow anyway, he was selling big talk. Why, I don't think it was any more than two weeks before that same cow was back in the auction ring. If Tom Hannah couldn't handle an animal like that, Walter Maxwell sure couldn't do it.

A Dry Cow
and a
Wind-Broke Horse

Do you know, telling that story about Walter Maxwell reminds me of a couple of other animals the man bought one time. I guess this must have been back in the late forties or maybe early fifties. I was driving my old black Ford then. That's how I can remember. Walter had a pickup just like mine, and since I bought a new Chevy in 1955, this had to be before then.

I know it was in the spring 'cause I'd gone up there to see a new colt Walter had. I pulled into his yard just after he'd got home from buying a crossbred shorthorn cow and calf over at the livestock sale at New Cambridge. I could see him backing his truck up to this old run-down corral he had as I came in the driveway.

I didn't know what he had in the truck, but I headed right over to check out what he was unloading before he let it out. I thought he might have something in there I could trade him for. As soon as I laid eyes on that pair of critters from New Cambridge, though, I knew something was amiss.

It was a nice enough little calf, but it didn't go with the cow. Walter was probably so intent on trying to get the best of somebody that he didn't notice he was buying a dry cow and an orphan

77

calf. Instead of turning that pair out into the pasture like he'd figured on, Walter was going to have to bucket feed the calf for a month. And he'd have had to use store-bought milk replacer for it too.

Of course, I've made lots of mistakes myself over the years. I remember this one horse I came across outside the sale yard over in Sand Creek. Now I hardly ever went all the way up to Sand Creek for a sale, maybe just once a year or so. It was usually when I had a lot of horses that I didn't want to sell close to home. Once in awhile I guess I'd even drive up that way to buy stock if I needed something I couldn't get around Deer River. It was a long trip, but I liked the Sand Creek sale. They had a special horse auction every other Friday all year long that was almost always a good sale.

This particular day, though, the auction had already started and I was walking around the pens looking at some of the live-stock. I can remember that I was particularly interested in this big gray gelding, because while I was looking at him who should come walking up but Mac Arnsted. I don't have a clue what he was doing clear up in that Sand Creek country. Mac didn't usually wander that far from home. That darn Mac, though. Right away he told me that he'd been fixing to buy the horse I was looking at. "But if you want him, Sparky," he said, "I won't bid against you. You can buy me a cup of coffee some day to even the score."

Now anybody who knew Mac Arnsted knows that he would've bid against his own mother if there was something he wanted at an auction and he could get it for a nickel less than he could someplace else. I told him that he could bid on any horse he wanted—and then buy me a cup of coffee.

Just then, though, this old fellow rolls in, driving a pickup truck, pulling a horse trailer. You could see the top of a horse's head sticking up over the side of the trailer so I knew it was a good sized animal in there. I didn't know who the guy driving was, although Mac waved hello to him so I figured that the old fellow must have been some friend of his.

The old guy pulled his truck up beside the corrals, right next to where Mac and I were standing. He was wearing a beat-up old cowboy hat and sporting about three days' worth of shaggy beard. There was an old woman sitting next to him in the truck who looked to be about the same age, and from what I could see she looked just about as scraggly as the old man. The best thing about her, though, was that she was wearing a cowboy hat that looked to be older than the both of 'em put together. It looked more like something that you'd want to sit on than put on your head.

The old man leaned out the window of the truck and asked us if the sale had already started. When I told him that it had, he asked how much livestock was being sold that day. Well, of course, neither Mac nor I had any idea about that, so Mac said that we hadn't got around to counting 'em yet. Sand Creek always had big sales, though, so I told the fellow that if he was planning on trading his horse, he'd have a long wait, 'cause there were a lot of critters for sale there ahead of him.

When I said that the old lady said, "See there, Dad. We might as well take Jupiter home with us."

The old boy didn't pay any attention to her, though. He got down out of the truck, complaining because he thought the Sand Creek sale started three hours later than it did. Then he climbed up on the trailer, and looked over the top at his horse.

"I couldn't interest you gentlemen in a good saddle pony, could I?" he said. "We don't have time to wait around at no sale."

Well, I always figured that if somebody had a horse for sale, the least I could do was look it over and consider buying it, although I always preferred trading to cash money deals. I climbed up on the trailer and looked in at what appeared to be a pretty good riding horse. I checked the cups in his teeth and figured he was only about ten years old, maybe a little more. The old fellow said that he wanted a hundred and fifty dollars for him.

Now this was a few years ago and at that time a hundred and fifty dollars was a pretty steep price for a common saddle horse. This was a pretty good looking animal, though, and on first glance you could see that he might be worth something like that kind of money to the right buyer. I looked the horse over a little more. When I got down off the truck I told the guy I couldn't go higher than about seventy-five dollars.

Well, the old lady heard me make the offer, and she yelled

out the truck window at the old man that she wasn't going to see Jupiter sold for that kind of price, no matter how much he wanted the money. She told the old boy to get back in the truck and take 'em both home. Then she sat there mumbling to herself while the old man tried to convince me to offer a little more cash.

He opened up the trailer and took the horse out and walked him up and down in front of me. Finally he said that he'd take a hundred and twenty-five dollars for him. Well, I went over and looked the animal over a little more, walking him up and down in the little bit of room we had there by the auction corrals. I could see the old guy was really getting desperate to sell him.

"Okay," he said. "I'll take a hundred dollars, but that's the best that I can do for you."

Well, this was a pretty good looking horse, and I got to figuring that I could sell it to Tom Hannah, so I told the old man I'd split the difference with him and give him eighty-five dollars.

The old guy thought for a minute, and then he took me aside and said, "Listen, how about ninety bucks so that I can tell the old woman that you give me a hundred."

Well, when he said that I laughed right out loud. But how can you argue against that kind of logic? I gave the old guy ninety dollars and took the horse.

As I watched the pickup drive away, though, I asked Mac who the old couple were. And what do you think, Mac said that he'd never seen 'em before in his life. He said that the only reason he had waved hello to 'em when he saw 'em was because the old guy had waved to him first.

Now, I'll tell you what, thinking Mac knew that old couple was just my first mistake. I took that horse home and put a saddle on him, intending to give him a little workout, but things didn't go anything like I had planned.

I ran that horse up and down the road in front of the house a couple of times, and then was just turning him around by my front gate when all of a sudden the poor devil took a coughing fit and went snorting and wheezing like he would never get his breath back. I got down off his back and tried to help him, but there wasn't a thing I could do.

After awhile he calmed down a bit, still wheezing, but nothing like he'd been a-doing. I had an idea what was wrong with him all right, and when I looked down on the road where he was standing, I found two pieces of sponge where he'd snorted 'em when he first went into his coughing fit.

That cinched it. I knew then for sure that I'd gone and bought myself a wind-broke horse. That's a horse that has the heaves. The heaves is a lung disease that leaves an animal breathing hard, even when they just do a little bit of running around. A horse with the heaves is no good to anybody and the old couple at Sand Creek had passed one off on me by stuffing each side of his nose with a piece of sponge.

That's an old horse trader's trick that makes an animal breathe through his mouth so you won't notice the wheezing. It's why a smart trader always looks at a horse's nose after he checks the teeth. I don't know why I didn't do that for Jupiter. I guess the old guy just got me a little off guard, especially with that woman sitting there in the truck complaining that she didn't want the horse sold in the first place.

Now I sure didn't need any wind-broke horse so I just decided that I'd take him right back up to Sand Creek for their next horse auction. I did too, and since I figured I might be able to buy me a couple of other horses while I was there, I picked out a good seat right down by the auction ring.

I guess I'd sat there about half an hour before I noticed the old guy who'd sold me the horse two weeks before. He was sitting on the other side of the bleachers right down in the front just the way I was. The old lady was right there beside him, too, still wearing her cowboy hat.

Just about the time I noticed them two sitting there, my wind-broke horse came into the auction ring. He was breathing hard, wheezing just like he'd run all the way to Sand Creek from Deer River. The auctioneer took one look at him and said, "Well, if it ain't old Jupiter again."

About half the people in the sale barn laughed, and then the auctioneer said, "Well, who'll give me a bid on him?"

From across the way, the old guy that I'd bought him from spoke up first. "I give you twenty-five dollars for him the last time," he said, "so I guess I could give you the same again this time."

Everybody laughed again and the auctioneer yelled, "Sold."
I knew right then the old pair were planning to use the same
trick they'd pulled on me to unload Jupiter on some other un-
suspecting fool—and make a few bucks in the process, of course.
They'd have to give somebody else the horse trading lesson,
though. I'd already learned mine.

Yes, sir. I lost out pretty bad on that deal. And that's not the
only time either. I used to figure that if I could make fifteen percent on everything I bought or traded for, I'd be doing just fine.
But there were always times when the trading wouldn't work out
the way I figured it should. I've sold horses where I didn't make
a dime, and I've sold just as many where I lost money. Over the
long haul, though, I guess I've done all right.

You've just got to learn to watch out when you're buying a
horse. That's all there is to it. Getting that wind-broke animal
turned out to be part of my education, and the money I lost on
him was my tuition.

See, there's no end to the things you have to look out for when
you're buying livestock. You can't take somebody else's word
about it. You have to look an animal over by yourself, find out
what it's like. Otherwise you're going to get cleaned, and it's like
my Grandpa Anderson always told me, there ain't nobody smart
enough to never get cleaned.

Cutting Stumps
and Plowing
Rattlesnake Hill

Yes, sir, there used to be a lot of horse trading done in this town. And we used to have some pretty sharp traders right around Deer River, too. There were all kinds of people, for that matter. Some real characters used to live in this town, that's for sure.

I don't think it's that way so much anymore, though. These days it seems like people everywhere are turning out pretty much the same. I guess it's just part of modern life, the way people are raised now. It seems like kids these days get sent off to government day care centers as soon as they can walk, and then to nursery schools, and kindergartens, and consolidated grade schools. Then they're off to high schools and universities.

Why, after all of that it shouldn't be any surprise that everybody's ending up so much alike. See, back in the old days a kid had a chance to grow up with less molding. Now I'm all for education, but them old country schools weren't near as bad as lots of people make 'em out to be. I ought to know. I went to one off and on for almost eight years. Back in them days, that's all the education you had to have. If you went any more than that they'd make you a teacher.

'Course, I know a kid needs more school these days than what we did. A kid today has to learn about computers and Celsius and all them other metric measurements. I know that. I just think people ought to realize all this organized schooling is hard on individuality. If it was up to me, I'd at least cut the education year back a few months, so the kids would have as much of a chance to learn about playing in the woods as they do about kilopascals. Six or seven months is all the schooling a person ought to have to put up with in one year.

I can remember one time back when I was in school, me and Pete Hawkins cut the season back a day or so on our own. Of course, it never seemed like we went to school all that regularly anyway. The school board always had trouble getting teachers to come out here back then, and there were two or three times we went a whole year without having classes, 'cause there was nobody they could get to run 'em.

One year, though, they got a good teacher for us and we went to school right up until the first part of May. I remember the weather was real warm that year, and one morning before school Pete and his brother Jim caught a skunk in a muskrat trap they'd set by the chicken coop.

Now they should have just gone ahead and killed that skunk right where they found it, but of course they didn't. And it just happened that I came by that morning on the way to school. We spent some time looking at the skunk, of course, and one of us got the idea of scaring our teacher with it.

We had a pretty good teacher that year, too. I can remember that her name was Miss Osborn. She lived with the Arnsteds just down the road from the school house.

I guess Pete and I must have been about eleven or twelve years old at the time. Jim was two years younger. Anyway, after we decided to play our little joke on Miss Osborn, we got busy gathering up that skunk to take to school with us.

See, a skunk can't spray you just so long as you keep his feet up off the ground. Pete and I ran a couple of long poles through the trap chain, and carried the poor critter, hanging there squirming between us, down the road.

When we got to school, though, we found out we were the

first ones there. We didn't really feel like hanging on to the skunk any longer, so we turned him loose in the school house. Then we went and hid out in the woods until the other kids showed up.

When Miss Osborn got there she went right inside. Pete and I were waiting for a scream, of course, and when it didn't come we snuck over and looked in the window. And what do you think? We couldn't see the skunk anywhere.

In a little while Miss Osborn called everybody in to start classes, but there was still no sign of that polecat. I could smell it all right. The odor wasn't real bad or anything, but everybody could tell a skunk had been around someplace. Miss Osborn said that there was probably one under the back porch and not to pay attention to it, but I think a lot of that smell was coming from our clothes.

About halfway through the morning she opened the closet door and that skunk came marching out just as brave as can be. I don't have a clue how he got in there, but you've never seen a school house empty any quicker than ours did that day, let me tell you. I think Pete and I were the first ones out the door, and Jim was next with the whole class behind him.

The commotion must have scared that skunk, though, 'cause he set off his perfume. Half the class smelled like a skunk for a few days, and it stunk up the school so bad we weren't able to have any more classes that year. 'Course, there were only a few school days left anyway, but Pete and I thought it was a pretty good joke just the same. I guess missing those few days of schooling didn't hurt us none. I really don't think a kid should have to go to school when it's warm outside anyway. I don't think it's healthy.

Now, you take Mac Arnsted, for instance. I don't know if he ever went to school, but he was a pretty interesting fellow just the same. Mac was as frugal a man as I've ever known. Jake used to say that he was tighter than a gnat's ass stretched over a rain barrel.

But I'll tell you what, Mac had a gem of a farm about six miles up the river from town here. One of his boys still farms out there, or is it a grandson? Yes sir, now that I think about it, it's one of Mac's grandsons that's there now.

Anyway, I remember him—old Mac—telling me once that the secret to successful farming is to never spend any money on anything that you can get along without. He said that he never let go of a dollar for a tractor or any other piece of machinery unless he figured he absolutely couldn't farm as well without it—and then Mac said that he'd always wait for a year before he bought anything. That way he'd know for sure that he really needed it.

Mac should have added that if a man wanted to be as successful at farming as he was, it would help to work as hard at it as he did, too. I don't think he ever really saw himself as an exceptionally hard worker, though. It was just natural for Mac to go whole hog into anything he decided to do.

Just like buying land. All his life Mac kept adding a bit of property here and there to his farm. And before you knew it, he'd gone and built his place into one of the biggest farms around. I remember asking him once if he was trying to buy up all the land in the area and he said no, he was just interested in anything that bordered his property. He was serious, too.

People used to kid Mac about being so tight, but I think a lot of folks used to envy his thrift a little, too. They just told stories on Mac 'cause he was so honest about being careful with his money.

One story I remember Jake Peters telling was about a time over at the 4-H fair in New Cambridge. Jake claimed he was sitting in one of them six-hole toilets they've got over there while Mac was on one of the other holes.

Now I don't believe this story for a minute, but according to Jake, as Mac was pulling up his britches some loose change from his pocket fell out and disappeared down the hole. I guess Mac looked like he was going to cry at first, but then he reached into his pocket, and took out two dollar bills, and threw them into the hole too.

Well, when Jake told me that one I just couldn't believe it and I said, "Now come on, Jake, why would Mac do anything like that?"

Jake looked at me and smiled and said, "Why, Sparky, not even Mac Arnsted would go down that hole for twenty-seven cents."

Do you know, for a good number of years Mac and Betty had a pet crow out there that was about the smartest bird I ever did hear about. He could talk as good as Mac and they had trained it to go get the cows at night. That crow'd fly out to the pasture screaming, "Here Bossy, here Bossy," and them cows would come in just like it was normal for a crow to herd animals. And if any of 'em lagged behind a little bit, that bird would land on their rumps, and peck at 'em to get 'em to hurry up.

At one time the Arnsteds had one of the biggest barns in the whole district. It was huge, three storeys high. I remember Mac saying it was so big the pigeons in the mow would fly out of range whenever he'd go up there to shoot 'em with a .22.

Mac told everybody he had to build such a big barn because he had such big cows. He said that his cows were so big, that at chore time he had to have a stepladder instead of a milking stool. He said they were so big it took two dogs to bark at one of 'em.

Mac said that he had one cow that was even too big for the bull. He said that when she came in season, he had to dig a hole for her to stand in so she could breed. After three or four years, though, it got so she'd follow him around whenever she saw him with a shovel.

I remember one time when Mac came into Bert's with his foot in a cast. Everybody asked him what happened, and Mac started telling this story about how one of his big cows stepped on his foot while he was milking. He said it was a huge animal that did it, a big Holstein crossed with an Angus, and try everything he could, he hadn't been able to get her to lift her hoof up off his foot. He claimed she stood right on his big toe.

Mac said he even pulled and twisted her tail, trying to get her to move, but she just stood there like she was in a trance. He said he must have stood there with his foot under that cow for half an hour with nobody around to help him out.

When Mac told the story everybody in Bert's started laughing. Pete said it reminded him of how, over at the 4-H fair, they used to fill a pair of pants with straw, put a pair of boots in the leg holes, and stuff the top end under some cow that was lying down in one of the stalls. All the farmers would know about it, of course, but some city people would always come along and think the cow had lain down and squashed somebody.

Yes, sir, everybody in Bert's that day thought Mac getting his foot stepped on was pretty funny, but I felt sorry for him, 'cause I had the same thing happen to me once. It was a great big crossbred red and white cow that stood on my foot, though, and I had to bite the old girl hard on her rump before she ever moved.

Remembering what happened to me, I said, "By golly, Mac, what'd you do to get her off?" Mac just turned to me and said, "There weren't nothing I could do, Sparky, except go up to the house, and get the block and tackle so as I could hoist her off."

Another time Mac told me about plowing that forty acre field that he had bought from Flora McKenzie after Bill died. That's that field that's mostly hill right up against the old Park Road going the back way out to McKenzies'. They used to call it Rattlesnake Hill. I don't know if they still do or not.

Mac said he started plowing along the road there and just went around and around the field, and around and around the hill. I guess it was what you call contour plowing. That was back when everybody used horses, of course, and Mac plowed there for better than a week with a four horse team.

Around and around the hill he went. He said that, come the second Saturday he'd been in the field, it rained a little bit in the afternoon, but he kept plowing, 'cause he wanted to get the job done. He only had a couple of acres to go, and the rain didn't do any real damage anyway.

In fact, after a bit it stopped raining and just drizzled a little bit. Sometimes the sun would even come out, but then the clouds would roll in again and there'd be a little more drizzle.

Mac's rawhide harness was pretty well soaked from the rain, though, and what with there not being much sunshine to dry it out, the harness started stretching on account of all that moisture, and from the weight of the plow too, I guess.

It got so that every time Mac came around that hill, the horses were pulling just a little farther from the plow than they were the time before. Mac said every once in awhile, the lead team would even disappear completely around the corner of the hill.

He said that he just kept working, though, even though it

was so cussed cold and wet that he felt like stopping lots of times, and his harness just kept stretching more and more all the time. He said that he didn't want to come back on a Sunday, so even when it started to get dark he kept on plowing. He just kept circling around and around the hill.

Then all at once something snorted right behind his ear and Mac said he turned quick to find his lead team pulling right there behind him.

That story of Mac's reminds me of the year I hauled cord wood out of the national park. They used to give permits to cut trees in there back then. You could sell the wood to the railroad for a dollar a cord. That was real good money for those times. 'Course, there sure weren't any chain saws back then. We cut with a crosscut saw and an ax, and then we hauled the wood out with horses.

The first day I worked in the woods it was just the early part of December and the weather turned warm, so the snow started melting. I had a four horse team, and was hauling part of my day's cut back to camp, when the new harness started stretching 'cause of getting so wet from the melting snow. The strain from all the weight of the logs probably had a little to do with it, too.

Anyway, there wasn't much I could do about it at the time. I walked the horses back to camp, with that harness stretching every step of the way. What with the snow being so wet, that load of wood was just too tough to pull. Me and the horses made it back all right, but my load of logs never came out of the bush.

By the time I got back to camp it was too late to do anything about it that night, so I just left my logs in the woods, unhitched the horses, threw the harness over the gate post, and went in to bed. 'Course, since it was my first day in the woods, I was pretty tired and just a little bit sore.

The next morning I overslept. When I finally got up and got my face washed and my breakfast ate, why, the sun was already up. And do you know, by the time I found my way outside, why, the sun had dried out that harness enough so that it had shrunk right back to its original size. And what do you think? It dragged that load of logs into camp for me in the process.

I guess that year was sort of like the winter Clyde Boscum

cut fire logs off Handle Potts's bush quarter. Times were pretty tough back then, see, and Handle let the taxes go on the land awhile.

It was timbered country, out in the sand hills, so he didn't have a lot of use for that land anyway. The story started going around, though, that he'd let it go back to the municipality for the taxes. Well, Clyde lived out that way, and I guess he got to figuring that if the municipality owned that land, the timber on it was free for the taking.

Anyway, this particular winter, there was more snow than we've seen around here before or since. Seemed like it snowed every day all through December, and we had a fair amount of snow the rest of the winter, too. At home we had the driveway piled as high as I could reach with the snow shovel, and I used to have to wear snowshoes to the outhouse.

Then, when spring came along, we found out Handle hadn't lost that land of his after all. He had just owed some back taxes on the property, and over the winter he'd paid 'em off. Now the snow was so deep that year, that it was the middle of April before it melted enough so Handle could get back into the sand hills to see his property. Of course, he wasn't too pleased to find out that the trees were all cut. Everybody around figured it was Clyde who took the wood, but nobody could prove it, of course.

I probably shouldn't even say it was him now, except both Clyde and Handle are dead anyway, so it don't matter to 'em anymore. After he got over being mad, Handle always joked about it anyway. He said it was real lucky for him that there'd been so much snow that winter. See, he claimed that even with Clyde cutting ahead of him like that, the snow had been so deep that he was still able to go in and cut over two hundred cords of wood from Clyde's stumps.

Bad
Weather

Yes, sir, we can really have some snow storms out here all right. Sometimes it can get so cold and snowy, a person won't want to go outside for days at a time. One winter I can remember when the weather got so bad even the snowbirds were trying to come indoors.

I'll tell you what, though. There might be places with nicer winters than Deer River, but it's hard to beat summer on the prairies. It's almost always pretty here in the summer. Of course, now and again the weather can turn sour in the warm months, too.

There's lots of stories, of course, about bad weather on the prairies, hail storms, and blizzards, and all of that kind of thing. And it's no wonder you hear all them stories, either. See, when you live out here in the country, changes in the weather affect you a lot more than they do in the city. Just one storm can destroy a family's income for a year, maybe their whole livelihood.

Out here the weather's important, so if people aren't telling tales about it, why, likely as not they're busy trying to predict what it's going to do next. I guess over the years I've heard every kind of weather prediction there is. Grandpa Anderson used to tell weather by the way the chickens went to roost at night, and Jake always claimed that he could predict the next day's weather from the color of the flame in his forge. Lots of other people around here used to tell weather by the moon. And up at Austin there used to be a woman who could predict storms from the way dogs and coyotes barked at night.

Some people used to say that you could tell how cold the winter was going to be by how many acorns there were in the fall, or how much down you could get off a wild goose. And of course, there were all kinds of poems that were supposed to tell weather. You know, the ones like "A sunny shower won't last an hour" or "Rain before seven shines by eleven."

The only weather forecasting I ever believed, though, was the one that said a dry spell is always followed by a rain. Pete Hawkins told me that one. Another thing Pete used to say about weather on the prairies was that if a person didn't like it, all he had to do was wait a minute, and it would change.

As far as stories go, I don't suppose there's anything that gets folks telling tales more than the climate. Anybody interested in them kind of tales, though, should have heard my Grandpa Anderson spin yarns about the weather in some of the places where he'd traveled. I doubt if there's ever been anybody that told stories about bad weather more than Grandpa did. I'd say he even had Jake Peters beat, and that's no little job.

I remember Grandpa telling about this drought they had once when he lived down in Montana. He said that it went so long without rain down there one time, that there were fish two and three years old who had never learned to swim.

Grandpa said the dust storms were so bad that the crows started flying backwards to keep the sand out of their eyes, and when the drought got real bad, why, the trees started fighting over the dogs. And dry, why, Grandpa said it was so dry down there that the cows only gave powdered milk. He said that twice a week he had to go down to the creek to dust the trout for ticks.

And talk about wind. Grandpa told one story about a wind storm that came up when he was living down in Montana that blew all the barbs on a barbed wire fence against the posts.

Another time Grandpa told about a day when he was out

haying, and the wind came up and blew the spokes right out of the wagon wheels. The same wind storm went through his far pasture and blew every bit of the water out of an old slough he had, and when he got home the shingles had all blown off the west side of the house. He said it was the worst wind he ever saw except for storms at sea.

Grandpa told this one tale about a wind that blew up when he was sailing out in the Pacific Ocean. He said it blew so hard out there that they decided to drop anchor and try to sit the storm out. When they let the rope go, though, the wind caught the anchor and blew it straight out behind the boat.

Grandpa said that the anchor rope just sang as it came off the spool and the anchor flew along there in the air just like a kite. And do you know, that wind was blowing so hard I guess ten men weren't able to pull the anchor back to the ship. Grandpa said he finally had to shimmy out the rope and carry the blamed thing back on foot.

Another time he told a story about fishing at this lake out in Alberta. I think this was the same lake where he said that there were so many big fish in it, the poor critters barely had enough room to swim around during the day, and at night a lot of 'em had to come up on shore to find a spot to lie down and go to sleep.

Anyway Grandpa said he was out there this one time fishing with an old friend of his named Moses Krider, when a tornado came along and blew 'em both right out of the water. The wind was so strong it just lifted 'em right up, rowboat and all.

Grandpa said the boat kept its right side up and he just hung on to the oars as that tornado carried 'em along in the air. He said they traveled for miles like that. They even flew over the town where they'd rented the boat, and when they looked down, they could see all the people walking around.

Grandpa told me them folks looked so small down there, you'd have thought they were just little insects. Then the tornado carried 'em out over the local fair grounds, too, and do you know, there was a tournament going on and Grandpa could see 'em playing baseball down there.

Grandpa said there was another lake east of this town, and the tornado sat 'em down in it just as slick as you please. He said the trip was smoother than a buggy ride, and they didn't even get any water in the boat. He said he still had his fish pole held between his knees when he landed. And what do you think? When he pulled in his line, Grandpa had caught a nice sized trout. Do you know, though, to his dying day he maintained that he didn't know which lake he'd caught it in.

Grandpa told another story about a tornado, too. This one came along when he was homesteading down in Montana. Grandpa said that he'd been out walking his fence line when the storm came up. He said he was running across the field heading for the house when he first saw the funnel cloud behind him. And before he had time to take any more than about two steps, that cloud just scooped him up and Grandpa found himself in the middle of the tornado.

Grandpa said that actually it was pretty calm in there, although it was awful noisy. He said he was just floating along inside what looked like a long black tunnel, and he said that he could look up, and see blue sky out the top of it.

At one point, Grandpa said he saw a neighbor of his float by, sitting on a rocking chair doing her knitting. Grandpa said he waved to her on the way by, and after she got past he noticed that her cat was still sitting on the rug under the chair.

Grandpa said that he more or less figured that he'd never get down, but all of a sudden he landed in a haystack, and the tornado was gone. He said that where he landed was less than a hundred yards from his house and only two hundred yards from where he'd first been picked up, but yet he'd thought he'd been gone for fifteen or twenty minutes.

I guess Grandpa's house was still standing, but the chicken coop was gone. Grandpa said he looked all over, but he couldn't find a sign of it. He said the chickens were still there, but all of their feathers had been blown off, and one chicken had been blown into a gallon jug. Grandpa said she was a barred-rock hen and she'd laid two eggs while she'd been in there. He said she had her head poking out the top of the jug, just cackling to beat the band 'cause she was so proud of herself.

Grandpa said that after that storm, he found a piece of straw that had been driven three inches into an oak tree. The most amazing thing, though, was that the tornado had lifted his barn right up off the foundation, turned it around, and set it back down again on the concrete just as if the barn had been built that way. He said that the straw stack beside the barn wasn't even touched.

I can't tell you any tales about wind storms as wild as Grandpa's, but I've sure seen some windy days around here too. Why, one time I remember when a wind storm blew so much air into one of my truck tires, I was able to drive on it for twenty years after it wore out.

Then one time I had three-quarters of a mile of new barbed wire fence blown away by a storm that came in from Alberta. It blew away everything: the wire, the posts, even the holes.

Now I didn't mind losing the posts and wire, but I hated like the blazes to lose them holes. Putting in fence post holes is a lot of work, so rather than start over I decided to go looking to see if maybe I couldn't find the old ones.

Now, it's no easy job finding post holes. They're liable to be anywhere. I looked for darn near a week before I finally located mine. They were more than three miles from home, blown up behind a snow fence and stacked just like cordwood. They'd been ruined, though. The wind had blown 'em so full of holes that they wouldn't hold dirt any more.

It reminds me of the time Mac Arnsted got blown off his barn roof. He was up there shingling it or something, when this wind came along and blew him right off onto a straw stack.

That roof is three storeys up, and Mac was right on the peak when the wind caught him, but instead of being glad for the straw pile, Mac was mad 'cause he'd ruined the stack. Charlie Maystead saw the whole thing, and he said Mac came up a-cussing and complaining just like always.

I'll tell you one thing, though. Mac Arnsted was mighty careful about heights after that. Me and him and Pete Hawkins put the roof on the arena in town—not the arena they got today, but the old one, the one that burned down back in the fifties. It used to sit right across the street from the Co-op grain elevator over where the new lumber yard is now.

I'll admit that arena had a pretty steep roof on it all right, but Mac was especially scared up there, I guess mostly 'cause I kept harassing him all the time.

Every chance I got I'd reach over and give him a little shove. Mac was older than me, but he was a pretty big man. I'd have never been able to push him around like that down on the ground.

Up on the roof, though, he was too scared to fight back. Finally he went down, and got a rope, and tied it to an old John Deere tractor. He threw the rope up over the peak, and then came up, and tied the end of it around his waist. That way he felt safe enough to shove right back when I'd get to teasing him.

With Mac fighting back there was no fun in pushing him around anymore, so after awhile I gave it up and went down to get a drink of water. After I got down on the ground, though, I got to figuring I might just as well give Mac one more scare.

I went over and started up that old John Deere and let her run awhile. You know how noisy them old John Deere two cylinders were. There was sure no mistaking that engine. When I came back up on the roof, I asked Pete what Mac did when I started the tractor. Pete smiled and said, "Did you ever see fingers dig into pine boards like they were cat claws?" Mac was already down on the ground by this time. He wouldn't work with me anymore.

I heard this story about a guy over in New Cambridge who's supposed to have got killed, or sent to the hospital, after getting pulled off a roof that same way. He was working up on top of his house attached to a rope just the way Mac had rigged his, only this guy had tied the other end of his rope to his wife's car.

It was a hot day, and after awhile his wife came out the back door and called up to him asking if she could get him something to drink. Well, without thinking he asked her if she'd go to town to get some beer. Of course, the car was parked in the front yard, and she didn't know he was tied to it. She went to get the beer, and as they say, the rest is history.

I guess you've heard the story about the guy who was shingling his barn roof in one of these prairie fogs. He started in the morning with the fog so thick he couldn't see his feet when he looked down at 'em. He worked right along, though, because he figured he had to get one side of the roof shingled in the morning if he was going to finish the job before sundown. At noon he went in the house for dinner, and when he came back outside the fog had lifted. And wouldn't you know it, he looked up and discovered he'd laid shingles six feet past the peak.

Pete Hawkins always used to tell that story. He'd tell it about himself just as serious as if it could really happen. I'd laugh every time, though. It didn't make any difference to me if it was true or not. It was funny, that's all that mattered.

Jake Peters always told Pete that he should have had a fog cutter the day he shingled his barn. Jake claimed he could make Pete one for about twenty dollars if Pete would send to England to get the steel. Jake said there was so much fog over there that they knew how to make the right kind of steel for cutting fog.

Goose Mountain

That Jake. I'll tell you what, a person just never knew what the man was going to come up with next. I remember one time he told this story about a prehistoric dog. Jake said this dog was just walking along one day when a tree fell over and squashed him. According to Jake that's why, even to this very day, any time a dog comes to a tree, he'll hold up his leg to keep it from falling on him.

I guess that story must be true, too, 'cause when it came to dogs Jake knew all about 'em. I never knew him when he didn't own about six of 'em. As far as Jake was concerned, any stray dog who came to town could stay at his place. He told me once that he'd trained one to use a chamber pot. I never believed it, but that's what he told me.

Everybody said that Jake's dogs ate better than some people, too. I don't know if it was true or not, but Pete always said that if Jake was frying eggs for breakfast in the morning, why, he'd fry up a pan of 'em for his dogs, too. Pete said that he didn't know if Jake gave them hounds toast and coffee with their eggs, or not, though.

Another story I can remember Jake telling was about a dream

that he had back in the days before he and Helen were married. He said that one night he dreamed that he was at one of them school house dances we used to have around here all of the time.

Jake said that when he woke up from his dream, though, he found out he'd been sleepwalking. He said that when he opened his eyes, he was outside in his front yard, dancing barefoot in the snow, and wearing nothing but his night shirt.

The worst of it, according to Jake, was that the girl he was dancing with in his dream turned out to be the potbellied stove from his living room. He said that his arms were wrapped around that warm stove tight as if it had been his sweetheart. Jake said that he just figured he was darn lucky there were only a few small coals left in the fire box or else he would have suffered some serious burns.

I always remember Jake saying that what he liked best about living in this part of the country was how the land changed so much from one place to another. And I guess that's true. If it's one thing we've got for land around Deer River it's variety. West of town is open prairie, with as pretty a river valley as you can find anywhere. East and south of town the sand hills stretch clear to the border. And north of town you get into the Goose Mountains. But do you know, no matter what Grandpa thought of 'em, there's some pretty rugged land up in there, just the same. It's not good for much except pasture, but it's an interesting place all right.

Pete always said that the only thing the earth up there was good for was to cover up hell. 'Course, Pete didn't think much of any ground that wasn't being farmed.

Nowadays, of course, the government owns most of them hills. They made the worst of that land into a national park, and that's how we get all of our summer tourists around here. They come to camp in the park, and go fishing, and spend a lot of money. At least the government says they spend a lot of money. I ain't never seen much of it myself, though.

Do you know, in the early days of the park they used to let us graze cattle up there. Some of the ranchers that lived close by even cut hay inside the park boundary. Not anymore, though. Now them rangers want to keep everything natural, except for all of the tourists, of course. Tom Hannah used to say that tourists were just like starlings. They were all right individually, but if you got a flock of 'em together you had to wear a hat and watch where you stepped.

I remember one time Tom and me and Jake Peters were all into Bascum's Store when Tom was complaining about some nuisance or other the tourists were causing him. After awhile, though, Wally Conklin started taking up for 'em. 'Course, Wally ran the store then, and I suppose he used to sell 'em something to eat once in awhile.

I guess Tom would've liked tourists a lot better himself if they'd been in the habit of buying horses. Anyway, after a bit Wally was getting the worst of the argument from Tom about the tourists, and so he admitted that once in awhile a tourist can be a pain in the neck.

Old Tom just shook his head and said, "If you ask me, the pain's a lot lower than that."

We do get a lot of tourists around here, though. But why anybody'd want to pay money to go up in those hills to sleep on the ground is more than I can see. Oh, I've done my share of staying out over night up there, but that was back before they made it a park. I used to cut timber all through that country, and I've hunted in it a lot, too. I always tried to stay out of there in the summer, though. There's too many bugs.

Why, the mosquitoes up there are bigger than a lot of birds. There's been plenty of times I've seen one sitting on a fence post, and at first glance thought it was a meadowlark. I've even heard stories of mosquitoes from up there carrying off dogs and small children.

Jake told me once that one of them mosquitoes came down out of them hills during a big wind storm, and blew clear up to Hastings. The mosquito landed at the airport there at the edge of town, and some kid put fifty gallons of fuel in it before he realized it was an insect.

I guess you wouldn't have known old Walter Higgins. He died better than thirty years ago, maybe it was even longer ago than that, but he used to ranch over near where they've got the park now.

One time he told me that the mosquitoes were so mean up there that he used to have to wear tin pants to the hay field. He said sometimes them bugs would be so thick that you could swing a knife through the air and draw blood.

Walter told me that this one time while he was haying, two mosquitoes flew by that were so big that, as soon as he saw 'em, he took off running to the house so he could get his deer rifle. He said that it only took him a couple of minutes to get the gun, but by the time he got back to the hay field them bugs had eaten his horses and were flipping a coin for the harness.

Now, personally, I never saw any insects that big up there, but I do remember one night when the mosquitoes were so bad they were a-stinging us right though a canvas tent. It got so annoying, we finally took the camp ax, and clenched their stringers over as soon as they'd poke 'em through the canvas. After we did that to a couple of dozen of 'em, though, they got together and flew off with the tent.

Then there's another time I remember camping up in them mountains when the black flies got so thick that you couldn't draw a breath of fresh air without swallowing some of 'em. Towards evening, we started frying a beef steak over the campfire for supper when all of a sudden a bunch of them insects came along, and picked up that meat, and tried to fly off with it.

I saw 'em in time, though, and reached out and stabbed the steak with my fork before they could get away with it. Pete Hawkins said the only reason them critters let me take it back was because the meat was only half cooked.

That reminds me of the night I was up there camped for an early season hunting expedition, and I woke up hearing something hollering in the dark. It was a chorus of voices singing "Heave-ho, heave-ho." This was way along in September or maybe early October and I lay there under my blankets, trying to think what could be making such a sound. It was coming from the front of the tent so I finally got up enough courage to shine the flashlight out the door, and there was a group of ants trying to lift my feet off the ground.

Yes, sir, Pete and I used to do a lot of hunting up in those mountains. Pete was always teasing me about what a poor shot

I was. One time we came back home, him with a buck and me empty handed, and he told everybody that I'd missed so many deer that he'd felt embarrassed for me. He said that he'd felt so sorry for me that he'd even tried to help me out.

Pete claimed that after the third day of me coming in empty handed, he had actually gone out and caught a live deer and tied it to a tree just to give me a better chance at hitting it. He told everybody that he had taken me out in the woods, leading me to the spot where he'd tethered this buck, and when we got there I'd shot at it and still missed the deer. Not only that, he claimed that my shot hit the rope and broke it, so the deer got away, too.

Another story I can remember Pete telling was about a bear hunting expedition he claimed to have heard about up in those mountains. He said that everybody in the hunting party except one fellow shot a bear on the first morning.

Pete said that night back in the cabin, the poor guy who still hadn't got a bear took a lot of teasing from his buddies. On the second day, though, this guy went out hunting all alone while everybody else stayed back in the cabin playing cards.

Along about noon they were sitting there around the table when they heard this terrible screaming coming from the woods. They all jumped up to see what was going on just as their hunting partner burst in the front door of the cabin.

He was running at full speed, but he never slowed down any, though. There was a grizzly bear hot on his heels, and he just tore through the cabin, and jumped out the back window. On his way through, though, he yelled, "You fellows skin this one while I go back for another."

Ruby Maxwell and the Red River Stove Company

Oh, yeah, Pete used to be full of stories about those mountains all right. I remember one tale he liked to tell about an old
neighbor of Walter Higgins who probably handled that mountain country about as well as anybody ever did—or least ways,
in a different way than anybody ever did.

Pete always said the guy's name was Bud O'Donnell, although
I can't remember that myself. This O'Donnell and his family came
here not too long after the turn of the century, probably pretty
close to the time I was born. I was just a little kid when he and
his family were living up there anyway.

They made their living raising cattle and sheep, mostly cattle. Nobody could grow much up on that land, but these O'Donnells, though, they seemed to live even closer to the soil than
most folks.

They just stayed in this old fall-down, one-room shack with
no furniture to speak of. They never bought a thing they didn't
absolutely need, and they didn't socialize much with the few
neighbors they had either. They just kept raising these cattle and
I guess the whole family worked like there was no tomorrow.

Now the thing is, though, these O'Donnells never sold any

animal they ever owned except for the young steers. They kept everything else no matter how good or bad it was, unless maybe they thought one was going to die on 'em. Then, I suppose, maybe they'd sell it. Nothing else, though. They even got their bulls from their own herd. I guess they figured it was worse to spend money buying something, than it would be worrying about the dangers of inbreeding.

Anyway, they lived like this for quite a few years, with that bunch of cattle just getting bigger and bigger. This was open range country back then, and in the summer they just turned them cattle out to roam all through the mountains. I'll be darned if I know how they kept 'em all fed in the winter. They did, though, and one day after about twenty years of doing this, old Bud O'Donnell just came in from the field where he'd been working and told his wife that it was time. He figured that they'd worked long enough.

This was along about World War I, when cattle prices were pretty good. Old Bud took all them cattle and sold 'em, the sheep too. Then the whole family packed up the few things they wanted to take with 'em and moved away.

People always said that they went down to Toronto and bought a big house and didn't work any more. I guess maybe they could've too. They had a terrific pile of cattle, maybe not the best cattle, but there was certainly a lot of them.

Yes, sir, there's sure been a mess of unusual folks come out of the Goose Mountains over the years. 'Course, nowadays nobody lives up in there. A few summer people have cabins along the highway going into the park, but it's only down where the land starts getting better that you can find any real farms now.

Sarah and I used to go up there to visit Walter and Ruby Maxwell once in awhile. Their place used to border the park. Walter was never much of a farmer, but we used to trade horses now and again.

Ruby grew up on the other side of the mountain, up near Ashley. I never could figure out how she came to marry Walter. She was always just as nice as could be to anybody who ever came around, and of course, Walter was about two pickles short of a barrel, and ornery as a long-haired dog with a permanent flock of fleas.

I remember one year Pete and I went out to Calgary to see about buying some cattle. We were there better than a week, and for a joke we sent Walter a postcard. We addressed it to "The grumpiest man in Deer River."

When we come back we found out Walter was pretty sore about our card. He said that it wasn't us sending it to him that upset him, though. What really hurt, he said, was that the darn postmaster knew who to give it to.

Oh, I guess Walter was really a friendly sort of person if he knew you. He just liked to complain a lot, and he had his own way of doing things, that's all. Ruby was just the opposite, though. I don't think I ever heard her say a bad word about anybody.

It's funny how different they were. I remember one year Walter ran for the municipal council. I don't know whatever possessed him to do it. I suppose he was just mad about something, but anyway, when the ballots were counted he'd only got one vote.

I never thought anything about it at the time. I knew he didn't have a chance of winning anyway. Not long after the election, though, I went out there and Walter was mad as a hornet at Ruby. It hadn't occurred to me before, but of course, since Walter's one vote would have been his own, that meant that Ruby must have voted for somebody else. I guess he wouldn't speak to her for about two weeks.

Ruby got to be kind of the town historian after awhile. See, when she married Walter and came to live on this side of the mountain, she started keeping a list in this little notebook of hers, with the names and dates of anybody who was born, or got married, or died in this district. Of course, it didn't mean so much in those first years, but after awhile that little notebook covered a fairly good span of time.

After thirty or forty years that book was great for settling arguments. Sometimes when we'd be over to Ruby and Walter's visiting we'd get that notebook down out of the cupboard where Ruby kept it, and we'd look up names—just for something to do. It was fun remembering when people died, or got married, or had kids. Why, the next thing you knew, we'd be telling all kinds of stories about things that happened years before. Ruby and Walter were ten or fifteen years older than me and by the time Ruby passed away, that book went back way more than half a century.

One story I remember laughing at once in awhile out there was about the time Sarah and I threw rotten eggs at the passenger train. It happened just a few weeks after we'd been married. Ruby had invited us to come out to their place for a visit, and while we were there, Walter and I found three or four chicken nests up in the hay mow. There must have been a couple of dozen eggs up there, and Walter gathered 'em all up and took 'em to the house. He claimed they were still good because there wasn't a rooster loose, and he said they had to be fresh because he'd just been up there a couple of days before and the eggs hadn't been there then.

When we got back to the house, though, Ruby said that she had plenty of eggs, and Sarah and I should just take the new ones home with us. This was back before we even had our own chickens.

Anyway, it was after dark before we got away that night, and we had a ten mile buggy ride to get home. A couple of miles from the house, though, we were coming up to the railroad crossing when we saw the evening train coming from Hastings. I made the horse trot, and we went over the tracks well ahead of the train, but going over the crossing bounced the eggs around and broke a couple of 'em.

Now, there's nothing that stinks worse than a rotten egg and that's what these turned out to be. I stopped the wagon to get rid of them, and Sarah and I both jumped down to get away from the smell. We were laughing about it, and well, the train was going past just then so we started throwing the eggs at it.

It was a foolish thing to do, but I guess we were too young to know it. We'd laugh at the people we could see going by in the train as the eggs splattered against their windows. It took us two or three years to build up the courage to tell Ruby what we did with her eggs, but after that, every now and again somebody would bring it up, and we'd laugh at it all over again.

I remember Ruby had a railroad story of her own that she liked to tell. It was about one time when Walter had to take the train to Moose Jaw. It was a two day trip up there and back so Ruby fixed him a big lunch to take along. She said she had fried chicken and potato salad, pie and cake, a few sandwiches and a half dozen apples all bundled up in a paper sack. It was enough food so that Walter should have been able to get all the way up there and back home again without having to buy anything to eat on the train.

Ruby said she was in the back yard when Bert Higgons come along to get Walter to take him to the train station, and when Walter came out of the house, she sent him back to get his lunch out of the kitchen. She said she never thought any more about it until later that day when she went to empty the garbage and found Walter's lunch. He'd taken the garbage along with him to Moose Jaw.

Walter never thought that story was as funny as Ruby did, but he had to listen to her tell it every time she'd think of it. And sometimes, telling it would make her laugh so much, her face would get red and tears would roll down her cheeks. Sarah and I would laugh, too, mostly because Ruby carried on so much over it. She could laugh more than anybody I ever knew. I was sure sorry when she got sick. She died the year before Walter did. That was fifteen or twenty years ago now, but do you know what I thought about most at the funeral—her nickname. A lot of the old people used to call Ruby "Red." Walter did too.

It was a nickname she got when she was just a kid, but I don't think there were too many people around who knew how she came to get it, and I don't think she liked it all that much either. Walter told me once where the name came from, though.

It wasn't 'cause she had red hair. See, when Ruby was just a little kid living on the farm up there by Ashley, it was just like you read in books. On Saturday night all the kids got a bath in a tub in the kitchen. Now there was six or eight brothers and sisters in Ruby's family and they put that tub right up next to the kitchen range so they could get plenty of hot water as they took turns in the bath. There wasn't anything unusual about that. It was the way everybody did it back then.

Anyway, Ruby's folks had this big old kitchen stove. It was made in Winnipeg and the name of the company was stamped across its cast iron fire door. One night while Ruby was getting in, or maybe getting out, she bent over and backed up against this stove and branded herself. Red River Stove Works was the name of the company, but just the word Red come up in welts across her backside. It was just as clear as a printed page, though. Walter said the scars were still there fifty years afterward. 'Course, I guess you had to look in a mirror in order to read it properly.

After Ruby died I always meant to go up and see Walter and make a copy of her notebook with all them dates in it. I never did it, though, and I'm sorry now. I hope Walter had sense enough to put her name in it.

Talkin' and Tradin'

After Ruby's funeral I can't remember talking to Walter Maxwell but one more time before he died. I went up there to make him a horse trade. It was the weekend after the summer fair we have here in town every August.

I remember that because it was the year I won the ugly man contest. Charlie Maystead was the runner up. 'Course, everything was in good fun. It was to raise money for the Community Club. Walter, of course, couldn't let me get away, though, without a good teasing about being voted the ugliest man on the prairies. I can remember how sympathetic he pretended he was, telling me not to worry none about taking the prize. He said he was pretty sure Charlie would have won easy if I could have just kept the smile off my face.

Yes, sir, old Walter really got a kick out of that. He laughed at me the whole time I was there, but I finally traded a young colt of mine to him for a pretty roan mare that he owned.

I wanted Walter's mare because the week before I had traded a nice stallion to Jim Bishop over at New Cambridge for a horse that looked just about like her. See, I could sell the pair of 'em as a team for a lot more money than they were worth individually.

111

That's why I traded for that mare in New Cambridge in the first place. I knew Walter had one like her. I figured that if I could get his horse, too, I'd have a matched team. And if I couldn't get Walter's horse, I was willing to bet that he'd give me a good price for the new one I had. See, that kind of dealing is all just part of good horse trading.

And I sure enough always liked trading horses; just trading, period, I guess. When I was growing up, there wasn't as much money around as there is these days and trading sort of took up the slack. Why, it was as natural for me to be a-swapping something, as it is for you to go to some store in the city and spend your money.

I guess being poor got me in the habit and I been a-trading ever since. I traded for this here pocket knife only yesterday. It's a Case. See the brand here on the blade. You can tell this is an old knife because it doesn't have "U.S.A." up under the name. None of them old knives did. They didn't start labeling 'em that way until they began bringing in jacknives from Japan in the 1950s. After that they'd always stamp 'em Made in Canada or Made in the U.S.A. or Made in England, or whatever country the knife was manufactured in.

That's why if you're ever swapping somebody for a pocket knife, you should look and see if it says where it's been made. It's as important as seeing what kind of steel the blade's cut from, or if the handle's plastic or not.

See, the thing about trading is that it's a whole lot more fun than buying something out of a store. It's more than just getting stuff that's the joy of it. When you're in a trade, doing the getting is half the entertainment. It's like my old Grandpa Anderson used to say. When you're in a trade you're using your wits against somebody else's, and when your trading's done, neither one of you should go away disappointed, 'cause you both swapped for what you wanted the most.

That's the way it is with trading. You always end up with something that you wanted to have more than whatever it was you traded away. Otherwise, you'd have never made the swap to begin with.

I guess I've been in as many trades as any man around. One

time I even traded Mort Jacobs out of the pair of boots he had on his feet. I didn't really want the boots, I just wanted to see if I could trade him out of 'em. Mort had to drive his pickup truck home barefoot and I eventually traded the boots to Morley Parker for a shotgun.

It was just a little Ithaca single shot, but I don't remember now what I swapped that for. Pete told me that the next time Mort Jacobs came around I should try to get his pants, but I never did. Mort's pants weren't worth anything to me anyway.

Do you know, I've heard of people who used to keep track of their trades. Why, you'd think they were accountants taking care of money the way they acted about it. I never did any of that though. For one thing it was just too complicated. Why, you might end up swapping a horse you got in some trade along with something else you got in a completely different trade. Now how are you going to keep track of that?

Or maybe you trade somebody for a couple of horses and then turn around and trade 'em off in two different swaps. There's just no way of keeping track of that kind of thing.

And what about the times you have to throw in cash money for boot—why, you'd have to have one of them computers to keep track of it all. No, I say that if you're a trader, the only way to really know how you're a-doing is to wait and see if you're any better off at the end of the year than you were at the beginning.

I only kept complete track of a trade once in my life, and I only done that to see what would happen. See, Jake Peters bought some scrap iron from me one time, and I got him to throw in an old Hamilton pocket watch he had for boot. The watch didn't work, but I couldn't get much more out of Jake than I'd already got, so I took the time piece when he offered it.

The next day I traded the watch to Harvey Arnsted for a set of hay hooks. I didn't need the hay hooks either, but there wasn't anything broken about 'em so I figured I was better off. I just tossed 'em on the seat of the pickup and kind of forgot about 'em for a while until one day when I was driving up to New Cambridge.

The hooks were still on the seat there in the truck and as I was driving along, I got to thinking about how you could take something small like that and trade it for something maybe just a little bit better, and then take that and trade it for something even better, and just keep going until you had something worth a lot of money.

It's kind of like that old story about the fisherman who didn't have any bait. He went out and found just a little piece of worm and he used that to catch a minnow. Then he used the minnow to catch a little bigger fish. And he used that fish to catch a bigger fish. He just kept turning whatever fish he caught into bait, until before long that fisherman had caught a record sized sturgeon.

Well, the more I thought about it, the more it seemed to me like a man could do the same thing trading here and there around the countryside. I got to figuring that I could get rich just swapping up from a set of hay hooks. I kept thinking about it and thinking about it, and after awhile I decided that, by golly, I was just going to see what I could do with 'em.

While I was in New Cambridge I even had a chance to make a good trade with Mac Goodmans, using them hay hooks for boot. But I didn't do it, no sir, 'cause I wanted to see how I'd make out with 'em by themselves.

A couple of days later I got my chance. I was into Jake's again, and I traded him the hay hooks for two sets of big heavy gate hinges. I thought that was an especially good trade since it was Jake I got the pocket watch from originally.

It seemed to me that the way it had worked out, it was just as if Jake had traded his old pocket watch to Harvey Arnsted for the two hay hooks and I had got the gate hinges for free, sort of like they were some kind of a commission for looking after the deal. The best thing about it, though, was that I already had a good idea who I could trade the gate hinges to.

I knew Pete Hawkins was building some new corral fence so after I left Jake, I took a drive out to see Pete. And sure enough, he was out in the barn yard digging post holes and nailing up rails when I got there.

That Pete, he was the damndest farmer I ever saw. He was so particular it'd drive a sane man crazy if you had to work around him any length of time. He was examining posts when I came in the driveway, measuring the length between 'em and how high they stood out of the ground. He was being just as careful as if them posts had been the mitered corners in a set of fancy kitchen cabinets.

Well, I watched him work awhile, passing the time talking about the weather and asking him how he ever managed to get his chores done, spending as much time as he did measuring fence posts. Finally, I asked him if he might be needing some gate hinges, and when he didn't say he already had all the hinges he wanted, I knew that he was interested.

I went and got 'em out of the truck and Pete took me around back of the barn where he had a new bull to show me. He took a glance at the hinges and then asked me what I wanted for 'em.

I said that I didn't rightly know, but he kept pressing me. "Come on, Sparky," he'd say, "I must have something around here to trade that you think that you can't live without."

Well, I said for him to just make me an offer, but all we did was stand and look at the bull for awhile more without either one of us saying anything else about them hinges. Before long, though, Pete told me that he had better get back to work. Then kind of as an afterthought he asked me if I'd be interested in trading a runt pig for the hinges.

Now that didn't sound too good to me, but I asked to see it and Pete took me into the barn where he had a pen with about a dozen weanlings running around in it. Ten of them little pigs were up about forty pounds, but there was another one weighed about ten or fifteen pounds less than that, and another one with a rupture that was even smaller. You could see that the two little ones were already getting pushed around by the others.

As soon as I walked into the barn and saw those pigs I said, "Now, come on, Pete, you weren't planning on trading me that ruptured pig for those hinges, were you?" I knew darn well that he was, but he changed his mind real quick and offered to give me the other runt for the hinges. Now, I'll tell you the truth. I might've swapped them hinges for that little pig, but I complained long enough about it that Pete gave up and threw in the ruptured animal too.

So now I had two pigs that I'd traded up to from that old

pocket watch, and I felt pretty good being into livestock, even if they were only a couple of cull pigs. The first thing I did was take the littlest one up to Doc Andrews to get him to sew the rupture back inside.

I'd had Doc do that for pigs lots of times. It doesn't really make 'em any better, but they look better. Doc only charged me a dollar. Doc wasn't a real vet, you know. He just knew lots about doctoring. He farmed over by Sparta, but as the years went by he did less and less farming of his own. He built up a little business for himself, doctoring other people's animals. There wasn't any real vets around Deer River back then. Somebody told me once that Doc Andrews had been a human doctor over in England before he came to Canada, but I don't know if that's true or not. It could have been, I guess. He knew a lot about medicine anyway. He certainly didn't have any trouble fixing ruptured pigs, that's for sure.

About a week after Doc sewed him up, I traded the littlest pig to Morley Parker for a spark plug wrench, and five sacks of oat and barley chop. See, I figured on feeding the chop to the pig I had left.

She lived in a little pen by herself right by the garden gate so I fed her garden weeds and vegetable tops too, as well as any scraps we had from the house. I figured she wasn't costing me a thing to feed her, and the spark plug wrench kind of made up for spending the dollar getting the rupture patched up.

I guess I must have kept that pig a couple of months, maybe more, before I got a chance to trade her. By that time she was a good-looking shoat and I made a trade to Tom Hannah for a Winchester Model 86 lever action rifle.

The gun was in real good shape too. I always liked the 86s better than the 94s or 92s, but I had no more than got it home when I traded it to Charlie Maxwell for a John Deere seeder.

I cleaned the seeder up and traded it to Harvey Arnsted for an old Cockshutt tractor that took me the better part of two weeks to get to run right. Then I traded that tractor back to Charlie Maxwell for an Oliver that didn't run as well as the Cockshutt, but looked a lot cleaner.

As it turned out, I didn't even get the Oliver home before

I traded it to Oscar Hoppingarner for a Willy's Jeep. The motor in that Willy's ran real good so I drove it up to Jack McClain's place—he used to run the car lot in New Cambridge—and I was able to trade him the jeep for a real nice little Ford two-door sedan that was only about six or seven years old.

I was as proud of myself as could be over that car. And why not? After all, I figured that I'd got it for a pocket watch. But as luck would have it, it wasn't two weeks later that I went to an auction out at Matt Jeffers's place and Clifton Boyer came along with the honey wagon and plowed head-on into my Ford. The car was parked on the road right at the corner and Clifton was drunk again. Neither he nor his truck were hurt a bit, but my poor Ford was a total write off.

It would have been a write off anyway, except Clifton didn't have any insurance, and of course I didn't have any either, so I couldn't do much about it except bellyache. I knew that wouldn't do any good though. It was like my Grandpa Anderson always said, "Never cry over spilt milk—it could've been whiskey." I just went about my business and tried to forget the whole thing.

After that, I always figured that what happened to that Ford was proof enough that a man shouldn't keep track of his trading. It might be all right for when the swaps are going good, but when things start to turn against you it's downright depressing. I've still got that old spark plug wrench that I traded from Morley Parker, though. I kept it as a souvenir.

Yes, sir, I've always been a fool for trading, and as far as that goes, I guess for talking too. I imagine that's why all these young fellows around here get such a laugh out of calling me Old Windy. 'Course, what they don't understand is that trading and talking kind of go together.

You need to be a bit of a yarn spinner if you're going to do much trading. You've got to be able to get along with people and enjoy talking to 'em. That's what I always tried to explain to Sarah. Being a storyteller is just part of being a good horse trader.

Look at old Tom Hannah, for instance. He might have had a little different way of telling his stories, but he was always willing to tell 'em. And he was always my stiffest competition around this area for horse trading, too.

I remember one time when we were making a swap of two young pony geldings. Tom got to telling me this tale about a giant bee that went buzzing around his head one time while he'd been working in his garden. Tom said the bee scared him so bad that he started swinging his hoe around after it, and the bee stung the hoe handle.

And do you know, that sting shot so much poison into that hoe handle that the wood swelled up to such a size, Tom was able to use it for a corner post in his corral. Tom said the poison must have acted as a preservative too, because the wood never rotted for the twenty years it was in the ground. He said the only reason he ever took it out was because he built a new barn and moved his fence.

Do you know, when Tom finished telling me about that bee I asked him just how big that insect had been anyway. He told me that it was about the size of a dog, and so I said come on now, Tom, how would a bee that big get into its hive?

Tom just shook his head and said that he didn't have any idea. That was the end of the conversation as far as he was concerned. It reminded me of the time he was telling me a ghost story and I asked him if he'd ever really seen a ghost.

"Nope," Tom said, "but I had a horse that did once."

I didn't know what to say to Tom that time either. I suppose I just went ahead and told him a story of my own. That's generally the way it is with storytelling. One tale just naturally leads to another one. That's what I try to tell Heather, my granddaughter. I can't talk into a silly tape recorder for her. Storytelling isn't a performance. It's just good conversation.

You can see that by the way it's happened here today. See, I started in talking to you about one thing, and that led to something else. And now, why it's gone and lasted the whole afternoon.

I guess storytelling for me has turned out to be just like my Grandpa Anderson always warned me it would. See, over the years I've told so darn many yarns, lies, and tall tales, it's got so now that I believe most of 'em myself.

PHOTOGRAPH BY PATRICIA PIDLASKI

ABOUT THE AUTHOR

Ted Stone is a freelance writer whose work has appeared in publications as diverse as the Toronto *Globe and Mail* and *Blair and Ketchum's Country Journal.*

He has been interested in storytelling all his life and regularly gives talks on the subject at schools, libraries, and before community groups. *It's Hardly Worth Talkin' if You're Goin' to Tell the Truth*, his second collection of tall tales, follows the hugely successful *Hailstorms and Hoop Snakes.*

Ted Stone lives with his family on a small farm near Eriksdale, Manitoba. His interests include agriculture, reading, music, bird-watching, and of course, collecting and telling stories.